AF350910

Haunted Hearts

THE HAUNTED HEART SERIES - BOOK 1

YOUNG ADULT ROMANCE

LIA LUCAS

Haunted Hearts
The Haunted Hearts Series - Book 1
Copyright © 2024 by Lia Lucas
All rights reserved.

Book Cover and formatting provided by Trisha Fuentes
https://bit.ly/m/trishafuentes

No part of this book may be reproduced in any form or by any electronic
or mechanical means, including information storage and retrieval systems,
without written permission from the author, except for the use of brief
quotations in a book review.

ISBN: 979-8-3303-6999-7 (Paperback)

Published by
Ardent Artist Books
www.ardentartistbooks.com

about ardent artist books

➡ <u>**ABOUT US**</u>

Ardent Artist Books was established in 2008

We publish modern and historical romances once a month!

Get Your FREE List: Published & Upcoming Books
visit our website at:
https://bit.ly/3Wva4o0

* * *

➡ <u>**WE HAVE BOOK TRAILERS**</u>

Follow us on YouTube!
https://bit.ly/3W3xn7a

Like, Subscribe & Comment

➥ <u>WE HAVE SERIALIZED FICTION!</u>

Visit our website today to download one of our stories that unfold in bite-sized pieces!

Each installment is just 99¢!

https://bit.ly/3LsDpJL

* * *

➥ <u>LET'S CONNECT!</u>

Fuel your love of fiction with exclusive content and captivating insights from Ardent Artist Books. Whether you crave the thrill of modern narratives or the timeless elegance of historical fiction, our newsletter delivers a curated selection straight to your inbox. Plus, as a welcome gift, receive a FREE downloadable eBook:

"The Family Fix"
https://bit.ly/49BR3UB

contents

1
arrival at camp willowood

present day

The bus rumbled along the winding road, surrounded by a lush canopy of towering pines that seemed to stretch endlessly into the distance. Riley Parker pressed her forehead against the cool glass, drinking in the verdant scenery as it whizzed by. The fresh, earthy scent of the forest wafted through the open windows, mingling with the excited chatter of her fellow campers.

In the seat across the aisle, a lanky boy with a mop of unruly brown hair leaned forward, his eyes gleaming with mischief. "You guys have heard about the ghost of Camp Willowood, right?"

A hush fell over the nearby campers, their ears perking up at the tantalizing promise of a spooky tale. Riley fought the urge to roll her eyes, reminding herself that ghost stories were all part of the summer camp experience.

"Dude, no way!" a sandy-haired boy exclaimed, his voice tinged with both apprehension and intrigue. "What's the story?"

The lanky boy's grin widened, clearly relishing his role as the storyteller. "So, like, ages ago, there was this camp counselor who was totally obsessed with this girl. Like, *crazy* obsessed. She didn't feel the same way, obviously, because who wants to date a weirdo counselor?"

Riley couldn't help but lean in, her curiosity piqued despite her skepticism. She had always been drawn to tales of the paranormal, even if she approached them with a critical eye.

"Anyway," the boy continued, his voice lowering to a dramatic whisper, "the counselor couldn't handle the rejection. One night, he went completely nuts and attacked the girl in her cabin. She managed to get away, but the counselor..." He paused for effect, his eyes widening. "He killed himself right there in the woods."

A collective gasp rippled through the captive audience, and Riley felt a shiver run down her spine, though she attributed it more to the air conditioning than the ghost story itself.

"They say his tortured spirit still roams the campgrounds, searching for the girl he was obsessed with," the boy concluded ominously. "Sometimes, you can hear his eerie wails echoing through the trees at night."

A chorus of nervous laughter and disbelieving scoffs greeted the end of the tale, but Riley couldn't shake the uneasy feeling that had settled in the pit of her stomach. She had always prided herself on being a logical, level-headed person, but there was something about the story that resonated with her in a way she couldn't quite explain.

As the bus continued its journey, Riley found herself gazing out the window once more, searching the shadows of the forest for any signs of the restless spirit. Deep down, she knew it was just a campfire tale, designed to spook and entertain. Yet a part of her couldn't help but wonder if there might be a kernel of truth buried beneath the embellishments. After all, the world was full of mysteries waiting to be uncovered, and Riley had always been one to seek answers, no matter how elusive they might be.

RILEY STOOD UP, brushing muffin crumbs from her lap as excitement flooded her. The bus lurched to a halt, and a wave of energy swept through the campers like a rippling current. Windows slid open, and laughter and chatter spilled into the still summer air. Sunlight pierced through the trees, splashing patterns on the ground like a patchwork blanket woven with golden threads.

As she stepped off the bus, the rich aroma of pine trees blended with the crisp scent of the lake nearby. It wrapped around her like a warm embrace. She balked briefly, absorbing the camp's atmosphere, where rustic cabins stood proudly amidst towering pine trees, their wooden slats kissed with a hint of weathered history.

"Welcome to Camp Willowood!" their cheerful camp counselor called out, her voice ringing with enthusiasm. Her bright smile stood out against the muted greens and browns of the surrounding woods.

Riley felt the sun's rays dance on her skin as she squinted, taking in the sprawling grounds. The lake shimmered in the late morning light, its surface reflecting a canvas of blues and greens. Birds chirped melodically, flitting from branch to branch, their lively tunes merging into a chorus that echoed in the back of her mind. This was nature at its finest, exuding life in a way that books could only hint at.

A group of raucous campers dashed past her, racing toward the water, their squeals of laughter blending with the rustling leaves overhead. Riley's heart raced alongside them, the thrill of old memories sparking within her. She had always been a little cautious, but here was a chance to embrace adventure—her last summer before senior year and a chance to break out of her self-imposed shell.

"Hey, are you coming?" One of the campers turned to her, eyes wide with excitement.

"Yeah, I'll be right there!" Riley called back, but her feet remained glued to the spot. She was captivated by the magic of it all—the way the sun glinted off the lake, the rustling of trees, and the ethereal beauty of the moment.

"C'mon, Riles," her friend Tanya nudged her. "It's just a lake!"

Riley huffed a laugh, shaking her head. "I'm not worried about the water."

Tanya rolled her eyes, already sprinting toward the shore. Riley turned her gaze to a figure standing off to the side, leaning against a rustic wooden railing. He was tall, with sandy brown hair tousled in a way that seemed effortless, sun-kissed skin shimmering with summer warmth. Even at some distance, she could see the playful glint in his bright blue eyes.

"Who's that?" Tanya whispered, nudging her sharply.

"Uh, just a counselor?" Riley caught herself stuttering, as if searching for words to cage her thoughts.

Tanya waved a hand dismissively. "Just a counselor? That's Ethan Jones!" she gushed, her eyes sparkling with glee. "He's a total heartthrob."

Riley felt her cheeks flush but quickly buried the warmth beneath her pragmatic facade. She took a step closer, her heart thrumming in her chest. Ethan stood relaxed, his posture easygoing, radiating a magnetic charm while effortlessly commanding attention from the campers around him. He laughed easily, his smile lighting up the air like the sun breaking through a cloud. Yet it was something deeper beneath those striking blue eyes that tugged at her—the hint of an untold story, an allure that made her instinctively pull back.

Amidst her curiosity, a chill ran down her spine. The ghost stories echoed in her mind, reminding her of the camp's haunted reputation. Caution whispered at her as she observed Ethan's ease—was it all just a façade?

"Let's go say hi," Tanya's determination broke through Riley's contemplative haze.

Before Riley could voice her hesitation, Tanya grabbed her wrist, dragging her toward the crowd that now swarmed around Ethan, eager for his attention. Riley's heart raced in rhythm with her footsteps, and she couldn't shake the mounting excitement mixed with dread.

"Hey, everyone!" Ethan's voice rolled over the noisy campers, steady and inviting. His presence commanded the area like an unassuming king. "Welcome to Camp Willowood! We've got a summer of fun planned for you."

As excitement pulsed through the sea of teenagers, Riley wrestled with herself. She wanted to be captivated. She did. Yet, something nagged at the back of her thoughts, the weight of her belief in the camp's lore holding her back.

"Riley!" Tanya's voice pierced through her internal tumult.

With a start, she shook off the thoughts and forced a smile, stepping closer to where Ethan stood. His gaze met hers, and her breath caught in her throat. There was something in the way he looked at her, unsettling yet enchanting, as if he'd peeled back layers to see the person beneath.

"Have you all settled in?" he asked the group, his tone easy and friendly, radiating warmth like sunbeams filtering through branches.

"Yeah!" Tanya bubbled forth. "But we want to know—are those stories about the camp being haunted true?"

Laughter erupted from some of the campers, but Riley's heart skipped a beat. Ethan's expression shifted slightly, a shadow of something serious flitting across his face for just a moment.

"We like to keep the camp's history a mystery," he replied, a charming smile returning as he leaned forward, eager to engage. "But you're all welcome to explore the stories and decide for yourselves."

A chill traces around Riley again, and she felt an electric tingle sparking between them as he spoke. This was it—a chance to dive into whatever mystery awaited her and perhaps piece together something real amid the camp's enchanting chaos.

"And as you explore, don't forget to have fun! I'm looking forward to seeing what stories you all create this summer,"

Ethan concluded, effortlessly captivating the room once more.

Riley felt her resolve waver, the tight knot of trepidation loosening just a little as laughter filled her chest.

Tanya nudged her again. "See? He's just a counselor. Trust me! This summer is going to be epic!"

Riley forced herself to respond with enthusiasm, shaking off the mystical chill still creeping along her spine. Sure, she'd come for adventure, and she absolutely would—if she could only ignore the strange energy weaving around Ethan and the whispers of the past that stirred within her.

* * *

RILEY'S HEART fluttered as she lugged her duffel bag towards the weathered wooden cabin. The scent of pine and campfire smoke clung to the warm summer breeze, beckoning her deeper into the Willowood experience. A mixture of excitement and apprehension bubbled within her.

As she stepped inside the rustic cabin, she was greeted by a chorus of laughter and introductions. Three other girls around her age, all strangers for now, eyed her with a blend of curiosity and friendliness.

"You must be Riley," a petite blonde girl chirped, bounding

over to her. "I'm Jenna. We're going to be cabinmates this summer!"

Riley couldn't help but smile at Jenna's infectious enthusiasm. "Nice to meet you," she replied, already feeling the camaraderie forming.

The other two girls joined the fray, exchanging names and hometowns with a palpable eagerness to forge new bonds. Melanie, a tall, athletic-looking brunette, and Sophie, a soft-spoken redhead, radiated warmth and openness.

As they settled onto their respective bunks, staking their claims, the conversation inevitably turned to the ghost stories swirling around Camp Willowood. Jenna's eyes sparkled with intrigue as she launched into a dramatic retelling of the tale she'd heard on the bus ride, about a counselor who died under mysterious circumstances decades ago.

"They say his spirit haunts these very woods," she whispered, her voice dropping to an ominous hush. "Seeking vengeance or perhaps... a connection to the living world."

Melanie scoffed, unfazed. "Come on, that's just a silly campfire story to spook the newbies. I'm not buying into that ghost nonsense." Yet, even as she dismissed the lore, a glimmer of hesitation flickered across her face.

Sophie, however, seemed captivated by the idea. "I think it's kind of romantic, in a tragic way," she mused wistfully.

"Imagine being so tethered to this realm, unable to move on."

Riley remained contemplative, her mind churning with a mix of skepticism and curiosity. As an avid reader of paranormal fiction, she had a deep fascination with the supernatural, yet her rational side couldn't help but question the validity of such tales.

Before she could weigh in, the resonant sound of a conch shell echoed across the campgrounds, summoning them to the central fire pit for orientation. Riley's breath caught in her throat as she spotted Ethan, the counselor she'd had an instant connection with upon arrival, standing confidently before the gathering crowd.

Ethan's welcoming smile and easy charisma instantly put the campers at ease as he launched into the camp's history and traditions. Despite her internal conflicts, Riley found herself hanging on his every word, mesmerized by his presence.

"Now, I'm sure you've all heard the stories about Camp Willowood being haunted," Ethan acknowledged with a roguish grin. "While we can't confirm or deny any supernatural activity, the tales do add a bit of mystery and excitement to our summer adventures."

A ripple of nervous laughter swept through the campers, some intrigued, others dismissive. Riley felt a shiver run down her spine, though she couldn't pinpoint its source.

As the orientation concluded and the campers dispersed, Riley lingered behind, savoring the last moments of the fading twilight. The shadows seemed to dance across the campgrounds, elongating and twisting in peculiar ways. A sense of unease crept over her, as if the very trees were watching, whispering secrets from a world just beyond her grasp.

Shaking off the unsettling feeling, Riley reminded herself that this was supposed to be a summer of carefree fun and self-discovery. Ghosts and haunted lore would have to wait; for now, she was determined to soak up every moment of her final summer before the responsibilities of senior year set in. With a deep breath, she turned and followed the path back to her cabin, ready to embrace the adventures that lay ahead.

2
the camp experience begins

The morning sun peeked through the canvas of Riley's cabin, gently rousing her from a deep slumber. As she blinked away the remnants of dreams, the unmistakable sounds of Camp Willowood drifted in—the melodic trill of birds greeting the new day and the distant laughter of early risers.

Throwing off her covers, Riley quickly dressed and emerged from the cabin, greeted by the fresh scent of pine and a hint of wood smoke. The grounds were already alive with activity, as campers and counselors alike ambled towards the central dining hall.

"Riley! Over here!" called out a familiar voice. It was Jess, one of Riley's cabinmates, waving her over from a picnic table where a small group had gathered. With a smile, Riley joined them, taking in the lively banter and easy camaraderie that had already formed overnight.

"Did you hear the ghost stories last night?" Jess asked, leaning in conspiratorially. "Apparently, there was this counselor who died here back in the seventies. Some say you can still hear him wandering the trails at night."

Riley rolled her eyes good-naturedly. "Come on, you can't seriously believe that stuff."

But even as the words left her lips, her gaze involuntarily drifted towards the dining hall entrance, where a familiar figure emerged. It was Ethan, the counselor who had caught her eye the previous day. His sandy hair was tousled from sleep, but he carried himself with an easy confidence that seemed to command attention.

As if sensing her stare, Ethan's piercing blue eyes met Riley's for the briefest of moments before shifting to address the growing crowd. A warm smile spread across his face as he raised a hand in greeting.

"Good morning, campers! Who's ready for the best breakfast of their lives?" he called out, his voice rich and inviting.

A chorus of cheers erupted from the assembled group, and Riley found herself swept up in the infectious energy. Whatever reservations or nerves she might have felt melted away in the presence of Ethan's charisma.

The dining hall was a hub of activity, with long tables lined with steaming platters of pancakes, sizzling bacon, and fresh fruit. Riley and her friends quickly claimed a spot, digging into the hearty fare with gusto.

"So, what do you think we'll be doing today?" Jess asked between bites, her eyes alight with curiosity.

Before Riley could respond, Ethan's voice carried over the din, commanding the room's attention with an almost effortless ease.

"Alright, campers, listen up!" he began, that familiar grin playing across his lips. "We've got a full day of activities planned to kick off this summer in style."

Riley leaned forward, hanging on his every word as Ethan outlined the day's itinerary—a morning hike through the wooded trails, followed by a swim in the crystal-clear lake, and culminating in a good old-fashioned campfire complete with stories and s'mores.

As the campers erupted into excited chatter, Riley felt a flutter of anticipation mixed with the slightest tinge of nervousness. She couldn't quite put her finger on it, but there was something about this place—a certain energy that seemed to hum just beneath the surface.

Shaking off the feeling, she turned her attention back to her friends, determined to embrace every moment of this extraordinary summer.

THE SUN CLIMBED HIGHER in the sky, casting a warm glow over the campgrounds as campers chattered excitedly. Riley stood at the edge of the swimming hole, where the water sparkled like a million diamonds spread across a brilliant blue canvas. It was a breathtaking spot, cradled by tall pines and bordered by smooth, sun-warmed rocks. The sounds of laughter, splashes, and the occasional shriek of delight filled the air as other campers jumped freely into the water.

But Riley felt a twinge of insecurity. The chill of the water loomed like an untouchable barrier. She glanced down at her navy swimsuit, suddenly conscious of how it clung against her slender frame.

"Come on, Riley! Quit holding back!" One of her cabinmates, Sarah, shouted from the water, a wide grin on her face. "You've got to dive in! It's awesome! Trust me!"

"Yeah!" piped up another girl from her cabin. "We'll race you! What are you waiting for?"

Riley contemplated her options as her friends bobbed and splashed around like carefree seals. She watched Ethan swim effortlessly across the swimming hole, his sandy brown hair glistening in the sunlight. The sight sent a flicker of warmth through her, making her feel even more torn.

"Just take a leap, Riles. You'll love it," a gentle voice said behind her.

Ethan treaded water, glancing at her with an encouraging smile that melted her hesitations. There was something infectious about his energy, and his confidence seemed to seep into her anxious thoughts.

Before she could reply, a playful urge surged inside her. *Riles? Cute nickname,* she thought. She pushed through the knots in her stomach and took a small step backward, gathering momentum. In one swift motion, she leapt into the air, arms outstretched, making sure her dive was swift and clean.

The cold water enveloped her, washing over her doubts like the shimmering ripples that formed from her entry. She resurfaced, slicking her hair back as delighted laughter escaped her lips. The shock of the chill invigorated her, and she spread her arms wide, embracing the thrill.

"Nice dive!" Ethan called out, swimming closer. "You've got some skills!"

"Thanks!" Riley beamed, feeling buoyant not just in the water but in her spirits too. She felt lighter, free from insecurities as they floated together. "It's all about the commitment."

"Right?" he chuckled, splashing water playfully in her direction. Their eyes locked for a brief moment, and an electric spark ignited between them. The air was charged with a sense of unspoken connection that pulled them closer.

"Let's see how fast you really are, Riles!" Ethan shouted, a mischievous gleam in his eyes as he challenged her to a race.

"Bring it on!"

As they lined up for the race, the other campers cheered, counting down with exaggerated excitement. With a decisive "Go!" they both launched into the water, arms flailing as they urged themselves forward. Riley focused on the strokes, trying to outrun Ethan, but every glance to the side revealed him gliding with precision.

"You're no match for me!" he teased, laughter bubbling up from both of them.

"Don't count me out yet!" she shot back, trying to match his pace.

The race escalated into a playful bout of splashes and laughter, each of them taking turns surging ahead and then losing momentum. Riley felt exhilarated; this was the most fun she'd had in ages. The water and Ethan's presence blurred any lingering worries.

But then, as she turned her head for another fleeting glance at Ethan, a sudden chill coursed through her body, a stark contrast to the warmth of the sun overhead. It was a feeling that gripped her like icy fingers trailing down her spine. A sense of being watched followed close behind, curling into the back of her mind before she could fully grasp it.

"Hey, you okay?" Ethan's voice broke through the haze of her thoughts, concern lining his brow as he floated beside her.

"Yeah." Riley forced a smile, her heart racing—not just from the cold sensation but also from the closeness of the moment. "Just a little chilly, I guess."

"Let's warm up then," Ethan reached out, playfully splashing water at her again, breaking through her momentary apprehension.

Riley ducked under the water to avoid the spray, popping up beside him, cackling like a child. She launched herself toward him to drench him back, throwing her head back, laughter spilling from her mouth.

They swam together, racing one another, taking playful dives beneath the surface, only surfacing between breaths of laughing gasps, as exhilaration tied them together in this moment. Riley lost herself in the fun, daydreaming of summer adventures and carefree days, every stroke bringing them closer as a competitive energy bubbled between them.

"Okay, last race! Loser has to swim over to that rock and back!" Ethan announced, pointing toward a large boulder sticking out of the water a little way off.

"Deal! You're going down, Jones!"

With renewed determination, they lined up once more, tension sparking in the air.

"Ready, set, go!"

They dove together, arms pulling through the water, legs kicking like mad. Each stroke was powerful, every breath deliberate. Riley felt alive as she pushed harder, wanting desperately to prove herself against Ethan. Just as her fingertips brushed the cool surface of the boulder, the air thickened with a sense of unease.

That same chill slithered down her spine, as if something lingered just beneath the water, watching her. A muffled sensation, pulled her focus into the depth of shadowy thoughts swirling around her.

She resurfaced to see Ethan not too far ahead, a confident smile on his face.

"Not giving up yet, are you?" he teased before glancing toward the shoreline.

Riley brushed aside her unease, rolling her shoulders back as if shaking off a particularly heavy blanket. "Not a chance!"

But even as she grinned, she couldn't fully shake the sensation, the threads of her focus tugged back to that strange feeling—a whisper from the shadows around them. As they swam onward, the laughter bubbled up between them, easy and free, the memory of their competition overshadowing the lingering chill, reminding her that summers were meant for splashes, laughter, and possibly a heart-stopping connection.

And yet, the water remained just a little too cold, the shadows a little too dark.

* * *

THE WARM GLOW of the campfire cast flickering shadows across the eager faces of the campers huddled together on logs and blankets. An electric undercurrent of anticipation hung in the evening air, thick with the scent of woodsmoke and roasted marshmallows. Riley felt her pulse quicken as Ethan's smooth voice carried over the crackling flames.

"Alright, campers, who wants to share a spooky story first?" he asked, his eyes sparkling with mischief. A few hands shot up immediately, while others shifted nervously, unsure if they were ready to face the night's tales.

Ethan called on a lanky boy named Jason, who regaled them with a classic urban legend about a hook-handed killer prowling the backroads. Despite the well-worn narrative, Jason's dramatic pauses and eerie sound effects had the group on the edge of their seats, jumping at every snap of a twig in the surrounding woods.

Riley became absorbed in the stories, even though they became more unrealistic. Her logical mind analyzed the details, looking for any truth or historical facts behind the folklore and legends. However, despite her practical nature, she felt an undeniable sense of excitement.

When Ethan's warm gaze landed on her, Riley's heart skipped a beat. "Riley, you're our resident paranormal expert," he said with an easy grin. "Why don't you share one of those creepy tales you know so well?"

A hushed silence fell over the group as all eyes turned toward her. Riley felt a strange prickling sensation on the back of her neck, as if unseen eyes were watching from the shadows beyond the fire's reach. Pushing the unsettling feeling aside, she cleared her throat and began to weave a tale she had read countless times.

"Deep in the heart of the Appalachian mountains, there's an old logging trail where travelers have reported seeing a ghostly figure wandering aimlessly," she began, her voice carrying a dramatic lilt. "They say it's the spirit of a young woman who was brutally murdered by her jealous lover over a century ago."

As Riley spun the twisted yarn, embellishing it with vivid descriptions and haunting details, the campers leaned in, hanging on her every word. The fire crackled and popped, sending embers dancing into the inky blackness beyond their circle of light. With each gruesome revelation, Riley felt an inexplicable chill creep up her spine, as if the very story she wove was manifesting around them.

Just as she reached the climax, describing the ghostly woman's anguished wails echoing through the hollows, a sudden gust of wind swept through the campsite. The flames danced wildly, casting eerie shadows that seemed to take on ghastly forms. Riley's voice faltered for a moment, and she could have sworn she heard a faint whisper carried on the breeze, like a disembodied plea.

Pressing on, she concluded the tale with the ghost's eternal search for her lost love, doomed to wander the mountains until they were reunited. As the last words left her lips, a hush fell over the group, broken only by the crackle of the dying fire. Riley's heart thundered in her chest, her breath coming in shallow gasps as she fought the irrational fear that had gripped her.

"Wow, Riley, that was seriously creepy," Ethan murmured, his eyes wide with a mixture of admiration and something else she couldn't quite place. "You really know how to spin a spooky yarn."

As the others erupted in nervous laughter and applause, Riley forced a smile, but her mind raced with a whirlwind of thoughts and emotions. Had she imagined the whispers on the wind, or was there something more sinister lurking in the shadows of Camp Willowood?

3
the first encounter

The night air was crisp and cool against Riley's skin as she stepped out of the cabin, relishing the solitude after a day filled with laughter and camaraderie. The gentle hum of crickets and the occasional hoot of an owl provided a soothing soundtrack to her thoughts.

She settled on the weathered wooden steps, drawing her knees up to her chest as she tilted her head back to gaze at the twinkling canopy of stars overhead. In that moment, the bustling energy of the day seemed to melt away, replaced by a sense of tranquility that allowed her mind to wander.

Riley reflected on the whirlwind of emotions she had experienced since arriving at Camp Willowood. The excitement of embarking on a new adventure had been tempered by the persistent whispers of ghostly lore that seemed to follow her wherever she went. She couldn't help but feel a twinge of disappointment in herself for allowing those stories to pique her curiosity, even if just a little.

After all, she prided herself on her grounded, pragmatic nature – a trait that had served her well in navigating the complexities of life. Yet, there was something about the haunting tales that ignited a spark within her, a yearning to unravel the mysteries that lay just beyond the veil of the ordinary.

Her thoughts drifted to Ethan, the charming counselor whose easy smile and warm demeanor had instantly captivated her. She couldn't deny the fluttering sensation that arose whenever their paths crossed, a feeling that both exhilarated and unsettled her. Riley had always considered herself level-headed, but Ethan's presence seemed to awaken something deeper within her, a longing for connection that she couldn't quite explain.

As she sat there, lost in her musings, a gentle breeze caressed her cheek, carrying with it the faint scent of pine and smoke from the evening's campfire. Riley inhaled deeply, savoring the familiar aromas that seemed to encapsulate the essence of summer camp.

But then, a sudden chill ran down her spine, as if the breeze had taken on a life of its own, whispering secrets only she could hear. She shivered, wrapping her arms around herself as she scanned the surrounding shadows, half-expecting to see something lurking just beyond her line of sight.

* * *

RILEY LEANED back against the cool wooden steps of her cabin, staring up at the night sky. Stars shimmered like scattered diamonds, and the crisp air felt refreshing against her flushed skin. She took a deep breath, pushing away thoughts of Ethan and buried ghost stories. The day had been exhilarating, a blend of laughter and sunshine, but now the calm enveloped her like a soft blanket, bringing with it a sense of introspection.

The night unfolded with a quiet serenity, one that allowed her to reflect on her fleeting moments at Camp Willowood. Fragments of conversations with her cabinmates flickered through her mind—playful banter and timid discussions about the camp's ghostly legends. But her thoughts kept drifting to Ethan—his easy smile and the way he effortlessly commanded the attention of the group. Just then, a sudden gust rushed through the trees, rustling the leaves and sending a shiver along her spine.

Riley shook her head, brushing aside the chill she attributed to the night air. She folded her arms tightly, glancing once more through the slats of the cabin porch. The atmosphere felt charged, as though the night itself held its breath. Then, without warning, a flickering lantern nearby sputtered ominously, the flame wavering like it was dancing to a haunting rhythm. She frowned.

"Okay, now that's weird," she muttered under her breath, eyeing the lantern. She shifted her weight, feeling her heart thrumming louder against her ribs. The rustle of leaves swirled around her, even though there was hardly a breeze. It was as if something stirred in the stillness, awakening an instinct deep within her. Her breath quickened, the eerie sensations pulling her closer to the edge of discomfort.

"Maybe I should head in," she thought, feeling the urge to retreat from the unsettling vibes. Just as she turned to make her way back inside, a coldness gripped her. It wasn't the friendly chill of a summer night; it felt more like the icy fingers of dread creeping up her spine.

And then she saw *him*.

A faint shimmer emerged in the night, coalescing into a figure a few feet in front of her. Riley gasped, her hands instinctively gripping the railing of the porch tightly. There he stood—a young man, glowing with an ethereal light, his translucent form wavering softly like it was woven from mist. Riley's breath caught in her throat.

"Whoa…"

The initial shock surged through her. Caleb's eyes were the first details that struck her. They were filled with a warmth that contrasted sharply with the sorrow that cloaked his presence. His mouth curled into a playful smile, yet the expression sent a rippling tension through Riley's chest. She felt oddly drawn to him, a gravitational pull that overshadowed her instinctual fear.

"Hey there," his voice floated toward her, an echo tinged with an otherworldly quality that created a knot in her stomach. "You're not supposed to be out here alone."

Riley's heart raced as she stumbled over her thoughts. "What the heck?"

He chuckled softly, a sound as light as the wind, yet heavy with an underlying sorrow. "I don't want to scare you."

Riley took a steadying breath, her hands still gripping the porch railing with white knuckles. She should have been terrified—after all, a ghost stood mere feet away, his spectral form radiating an otherworldly glow. But for Riley, encounters like this were nothing new.

Ever since she was a little girl, Riley possessed a unique gift that had been passed down through the women in her family for generations. She could see and communicate with the spirits of those who had passed on to the other side. It was a talent that her mother and grandmother before her had nurtured within her, never treating it as something to be feared.

As a child, Riley's nightly visitors were often loved ones who had died—grandparents, great-aunts, and even childhood friends taken too soon. They would manifest in her bedroom, their ghostly forms illuminated by the moonlight filtering through the curtains. While some might have been frightened by such apparitions, Riley's family had instilled in her a sense of comfort and acceptance. The spirits didn't come to haunt or torment; they simply yearned for connection and closure, seeking solace and sometimes even aid in moving on.

Riley's ability allowed her to bridge the divide between the living and the dead, offering a compassionate ear and a willingness to help however she could. Whether it was relaying long-unspoken messages to grieving relatives or providing guidance for restless souls, she embraced her role as a mediator between worlds.

As she grew older, Riley's gift only strengthened, and her encounters with the beyond became more frequent. She learned to hone her abilities, reading the subtleties in the spirits' expressions and energies, and discerning their intentions and needs. It was a responsibility she carried with grace and empathy, understanding that her role was to be a conduit for healing and acceptance.

So, when the ghostly figure of Caleb materialized before her on the porch of her cabin, Riley's initial surprise swiftly gave way to curiosity and a deep-rooted sense of familiarity. She knew, just as she had known countless times before, that this spirit had sought her out for a reason—a lingering attachment, a burning question, or perhaps even a cry for help that only she could truly hear.

"What… what do you want?" Her voice trembled, uncertainty making her question falter.

Caleb stepped closer, the shadows playing tricks around him, heightening the atmosphere. "I just wanted to talk. It's been a long time since anyone's been up this late at camp." His eyes conveyed a longing that cut through the air like a whisper.

Riley shuffled backward a step, her heartbeat pounding in her ears. "This always happens when kids tell ghost stories."

"Stories," he repeated softly, a hint of amusement in his tone. "Everyone loves a good tale, but I'm no mere figment." The way he moved was unsettling and mesmerizing, as though he floated rather than walked. "There's much to learn about the past. About me."

"Learn? About you," Riley echoed, slowly shifting her stance. The aura surrounding him was magnetic, compelling a morbid curiosity. She couldn't help but want to grasp the reality behind his existence. "What do you mean?"

His expression sharpened, the playful glimmer fading slightly. "There's a reason I'm still here."

Riley's stomach knotted. "Why? Did something happen? Did you die here?" Words tumbled from her mouth, curiosity overpowering caution. Gripping the porch railing tighter, she fought against the fear that buzzed at the edges of her consciousness.

Caleb took a step forward, this time more intentionally. "Yes… it's complicated. I just—I need someone to understand. To listen."

this ghost of a boy who longed for understanding. Everything within her wavered at the precipice of a decision, a leap into the unknown, a terrifying yet exhilarating dance with fate.

But for now, words escaped her, lodged in her throat. She stood at the threshold, an invisible line drawn between fear and fascination, unsure of which side she belonged.

Caleb's expression remained earnest, pulling her out of her spiraling thoughts. "The truth is waiting. Are you ready to find it?"

Riley's breaths turned shallow as time hung delicately, poised on the edge of their exchange. In that moment, she knew there was no going back.

CALEB STOOD THERE, his translucent body emanating a soft, ethereal glow that illuminated the night around him. At first glance, he seemed playful, a gentle smile teasing the corners of his mouth, but there was something deeper lurking behind his sorrowful eyes.

Riley gasped, her heart racing as she processed the apparition before her. He was breathtaking yet unsettling, like a haunting melody that lured her in, only to leave dread trailing behind it. Fear wrestled with curiosity; she found herself captivated by the ghostly boy, a whirlwind of emotion swirling inside her like a storm.

"Riley," his voice drifted through the air, soft yet echoing, like a grainy recording played too loud. Each word wrapped around her senses, both beautiful and disconcerting.

Riley instinctively took a step back, a stutter in her heart as she fought the urge to run. "How did you know my name?" her voice trembled, teetering between fascination and fright.

Caleb tilted his head, shadows playing across his features, accentuating the sadness in his gaze. "Your grandmother told me you could help. I'm Caleb," he stated, as if introducing himself in a normal setting, yet the weight of his words enveloped the air around them with a heavy solemnity. "I've been waiting a long time for someone to hear me." His breathy words shimmered like mist, thick with longing.

Riley felt a lump form in her throat at the mention of her grandmother. Memories flooded back like a torrential downpour, of the kind, warm woman who had been her confidante, her guiding star. Her grandmother's stories of spirits and the unseen world used to lull her to sleep, a comforting blend of the mystical and the familiar. But that was years ago, a chapter of her life she thought she had closed when her grandmother passed away. The mention of her name stirred up a potent cocktail of emotions in Riley's heart - aching loss, longing, and a hint of fear. The woman she missed every single day was somehow connected to the ghostly figure before her.

"How is she?" She crossed her arms, instinctively defending herself against the unease wrapping around her, even as her heart hammered in her chest.

"She's good," Caleb said, nonchalantly. "She told me to tell you she now has all the time in the world to play canasta."

A smile bloomed on Riley's face. Her grandmother did love her card games. "What do you want from me, Caleb?"

"Answers," he replied, sorrow creeping back into his tone like twilight falling over the sun. "There are things left undone—secrets bound to this place." He stepped closer, curiosity igniting in his expressive eyes, but the juxtaposition of his ethereal glow against the night cast an unnerving shadow over her. "You can see me, can't you?"

Riley swallowed, her pulse thrumming louder than her thoughts. "Yes."

"Then you must feel it. The history that lingers here, the sorrow." He extended a hand, translucent fingers reaching toward her. "You're different. You can help me."

"How?" Riley asked, feeling tired now.

"Tired?" Caleb's smile wavered, a faint echo of mischief playing at the edges of his expression. He floated a step closer, that pulsing energy drawing her in against her better judgment. "You've heard the rumors about this place … about what happened."

Riley wanted to press her hands against her ears, block out the compulsion rising in her. But his gaze dismantled her defenses. So intense, so familiar, as if he held pieces of her own hidden thoughts. Every instinct told her to run, yet there was a fierce pull—a magnetism she had never experienced. "I don't know if I can help you," she whispered, the truth of her words heavy like the atmosphere closing in on them.

"Yes," he replied simply, that sad gentleness radiating from him. "But I was once like you, full of dreams and laughter. Campers like you have whispered my name. Their stories became mine. I became the mystery."

Their proximity quickened the air, the atmosphere sparking with energy. The night seemed charged, the world around them fading, leaving only them caught in this moment. "There must be a way," he continued, an earnest plea shining within the depths of his swirling gaze. "You have something they don't—connection."

Riley's heart quickened. Connection? How could she possibly connect with a ghost? Yet she sensed the truth in his words, that unbreakable bond formed through emotion, tragedy, and unfulfilled dreams. "What if I can't help?" she hesitated, torn between the supernatural and the safety of her own reality.

Caleb's expression shifted, shadows softening, dark eyes pleading yet resolute. "You can, Riley. If you are willing to reach into the darkness." His voice trailed off, dense with an urgency that hinted at the weight of all that remained unsaid.

But the chill in the air was palpable, anxiety snaking its way through her veins. Riley wanted to move, to close her eyes and block him out, yet she found herself frozen, tethered by his gaze. The connection between them charged the space, different from what she felt when she was near Ethan—spirited electricity against Caleb's ethereal glow.

"Please," he whispered, that simple plea ringing true like the first promise of dawn. "I need to be seen."

The world around them faded further, encasing them in a hush that intensified each heartbeat, each flutter of hope and fear. Riley clutched her arms tighter, caught between choices she never anticipated, yet still powerless to step away.

getting to know ethan

orning light poured into the cabin, casting playful patterns on the wooden floorboards. Riley stirred awake, her heart still echoing the thrill and chill from the previous night. The sun warmed her cheek, yet a shiver ran down her spine as memories of Caleb's gaze flickered in and out of her mind. She brushed her hair back from her face, pushing away the indulgent thoughts of ghostly encounters, willing herself to view it as a figment, a trick of her imagination.

"Maybe he won't be back," she muttered to herself, shaking her head as she swung her legs over the side of the bed. But the memory lingered—a soft glow, an urgent yet silent plea. She couldn't quite shake the way Caleb had seemed to reach for her, his eyes a mirror of longing that echoed in the depths of her own heart.

The cabin buzzed with excitement as her cabinmates sprang into action, clawing at their clothes and gathering for breakfast. Riley slipped on a comfy T-shirt and shorts, grabbing a quick brush through her hair before heading to the communal dining hall. Conversations flowed around her, laughter spilling like sunlight across the tables.

The smell of bacon and syrup enveloped her as she sat down with her friends. They huddled close, sharing stories from the previous day, laughter mingling with the clinking of cutlery. Riley feigned interest in their enthusiasm, but her thoughts wandered away from her friends, toward a certain sandy-haired counselor who stood across the room.

Ethan effortlessly commanded attention, surrounded by a gaggle of younger campers. His laughter rang out like music, light and inviting. A couple of them leaned in closer, hanging on his every joke, and Riley felt a pang of envy at the ease with which he engaged everyone. He wasn't just a counselor; he was a magnet, drawing everyone's happiness toward him.

"Riley, earth to Riley?"

Her friend Sarah's voice cut through Riley's reverie, and she blinked, focusing on the table as her cheeks warmed uncomfortably.

"Sorry, lost in thought," she replied with a sheepish smile, but her eyes flicked back to Ethan, instinctively searching for that spark of connection.

"I think he's taken," Sarah grinned, elbowing her teasingly.

Riley shot her a look, half annoyance, half embarrassment. "Shut up. I'm just trying to enjoy breakfast. Right?"

Flushing, she aimed to redirect the conversation and divert the spotlight from herself.

"He's really good with the campers, isn't he?" she said, forcing a casual tone while stealing another glance at Ethan.

"Good? Try amazing," one of the other girls chimed in, flicking her hair back dramatically. "I heard he's been a counselor here for years! Total crush material."

"How old is he?" Riley asked, interested.

"I think he's like-what, seventeen? Been a counselor for-like, two years now?"

Riley rolled her eyes, but the warmth in her heart twisted. The twinge of affectionate competition stirred within her, rekindled by the sparkle in Ethan's eyes as he joke-battled with campers. She felt excitement bubbling alongside her confusion, a strange duality that kept her teetering between two worlds. On one hand, the tangible warmth and magnetic charm of Ethan—the living, breathing boy who illuminated the mornings; on the other, the ethereal pull of Caleb, a mystery shrouded in shadows and secrets.

"Oh, I think Riley has a little crush," laughed Sarah, winking at her.

"Please," Riley snorted, attempting to deflect attention. Her heart raced at her slipping thoughts. "I just appreciate good humor and skills. It's not… like that."

Eventually, breakfast wrapped up with playful shoves and plans for the day. Riley took a deep breath, telling herself to shake it off. The time spent with her friends was supposed to feel lively and carefree. Yet, even in the blissful undertones of laughter, her mind drifted back to the vision of Caleb, his sad expression juxtaposed with Ethan's effortless smile.

As they finished up, Ethan approached their table, a sunbeam breaking through the clouds of her thoughts. "Morning, ladies," he said, flashing them that smile that made Riley's heart stutter.

"Enjoying the food?"

"Always!" Sarah chimed with unabashed zeal, but Riley silently struggled to keep her composure under the weight of his gaze.

"You guys ready for some hiking today? I heard the views are amazing from the overlook," Ethan added, his enthusiasm infectious.

Riley nodded, her stomach fluttering. "Definitely." The promise of adventure shot through her, curiously linking it to the previous night's otherworldly encounter. She wanted to prove to herself that she could enjoy the summer fully and let the strange occurrences drift away like wisps of fog.

Ethan leaned closer, as if sharing a secret. "You'll love it. But you know, if you end up having a ghost follow you, I think I might need to step in as your ghost buster!" Laughter erupted as his joke found eager ears, but Riley felt the warmth pooling in her cheeks, an undeniable heat of embarrassment and intrigue that swept through her like wildfire.

"Yeah, I'll be sure to keep that in mind."

He grinned, and the world melted away momentarily. Suddenly, this was all that mattered—the warmth of summer, her companions full of laughter, and the prospect of adventure.

As the girls stood up to follow Ethan out to the hiking trails, Riley cast one last look back over her shoulder at their table. The memory of Caleb flickered at the edges of her thoughts, but she shrugged it off, determined to settle into the exhilaration of summer camp fun.

"Here we go!" Ethan exclaimed, leading the charge toward the trail, his laughter echoing through the trees as they left the familiarity of the dining hall. Riley took a deep breath of fresh pine-scented air, her heart racing with a mix of anticipation and confusion about what the day would hold. As she kept pace with Ethan, she felt, for the first time that morning, a spark of hope that perhaps this summer would bring clarity—both in her friendships and the mysteries that haunted her mind.

The trail beckoned ahead, each step forward a promise of adventure, the voices of her friends blending with the rustling leaves above. Riley's mind began to clear, focusing on the warmth of the moment, unaware of the paths that lay waiting beyond this bright summer day.

* * *

THE AFTERNOON SUN cast a warm glow over the camp as Riley and Ethan tackled their assigned cabin duty. Sweeping the hardwood floors and straightening the bunks, they moved in sync, exchanging casual banter that slowly chipped away at Riley's initial shyness.

"So, you're the resident expert on all things spooky, huh?" Ethan teased, flashing her a lopsided grin as he fluffed a pillow.

Riley felt her cheeks flush, but she met his gaze with a playful eye roll. "I prefer to think of myself as a connoisseur of the paranormal."

Ethan chuckled, the sound rich and inviting. "Alright, connoisseur, hit me with your best ghost story."

As they continued tidying the cabin, Riley launched into an animated retelling of one of her favorite tales, her voice hushed with dramatic flair. Ethan listened intently, his brilliant blue eyes fixed on her as she described the haunting details.

"Not bad," he conceded when she finished. "But you're missing a key ingredient—" He leaned in conspiratorially, their shoulders brushing. "The twist ending."

Riley's breath caught in her throat at his proximity, but she refused to be flustered. "Oh, really? And what makes you such an expert on ghost stories, Mr. Counselor?"

Ethan's gaze held a hint of mischief as he straightened up, grabbing a broom to sweep. "I'll have you know, I'm something of a storyteller myself. The campers can't get enough of my tales around the campfire."

"Is that so?" Riley arched an eyebrow, her lips curving into a challenging smirk. "Prove it, then. Let's hear one of your famous ghost stories."

For a moment, Ethan seemed to hesitate, a flicker of something unreadable passing across his features. But then his easy grin returned, and he launched into a chilling tale of a vengeful spirit that haunted these very woods.

As he spun the yarn, his voice taking on a rich, captivating cadence, Riley found herself utterly transfixed. The way he wove the details, from the eerie howls in the night to the ghostly apparitions glimpsed between the trees, sent delicious shivers down her spine.

By the time he reached the climactic twist, they had gravitated closer, their shoulders brushing as they leaned against the wall, lost in the story. Ethan's voice dropped to a hushed murmur, his breath warm against her cheek as he described the spirit's final, chilling reveal.

In that suspended moment, the air seemed to crackle with electricity, and Riley's heart hammered in her chest. She was acutely aware of Ethan's presence, the faint woodsy scent that clung to him, the way his features seemed to soften as their eyes met.

A charged silence stretched between them, thick with unspoken tension. Riley felt herself leaning in, drawn to him like a moth to a flame, unable to resist the magnetic pull.

Just then, the sound of approaching footsteps shattered the spell. Ethan straightened abruptly, clearing his throat as one of the younger campers poked her head in, oblivious to the moment she had interrupted.

"Hey, you guys almost done in here?" she asked, her voice cutting through the lingering haze of the story.

Riley blinked rapidly, snapping back to reality as Ethan responded with an easy smile. "Just about. We'll be right out."

As the camper scampered off, Riley couldn't help but feel a pang of disappointment. The intensity of that brief connection still hummed through her veins, leaving her flustered and breathless.

Ethan shot her a sidelong glance, his expression unreadable. "Well, looks like we'd better wrap this up."

Nodding mutely, Riley busied herself with the last few tasks, her mind buzzing with a whirlwind of emotions. One thing was certain—whatever this growing bond with Ethan was, it felt far more electrifying than any ghost story could ever convey.

THE SUN DIPPED below the trees, casting warm hues of orange and pink across the sky. Evenings at Camp Willowood transformed the ordinary into something extraordinary. Laughter echoed around the dining hall as campers wrapped up their meals, but all Riley could think about was the invitation she'd received from Ethan.

"Hey, want to take a walk?" He stood just beyond the entrance, the last rays of sunlight highlighting the tousle of his sandy brown hair and the warmth in his piercing blue eyes.

"Sure," she murmured, trying to appear nonchalant despite the flurry of butterflies in her stomach. As they stepped out into the dusk, the sounds of the camp began to soften, turning the world into a pocket of tranquility.

The path wound through tall pines, their needles whispering secrets as a gentle evening breeze rustled through them. Stars began to prick the twilight canvas above them, revealing themselves one by one.

"What a perfect night," Ethan said, stuffing his hands into the pockets of his shorts and glancing up at the sky. His relaxed demeanor reassured Riley, easing some of the tension coiling in her stomach.

"Yeah, it really is." She inhaled deeply, the earthy scent of the forest mingling with the sweetness of summer blossoms. They walked side by side, the distance between them shrinking with every step.

"What are you hoping to get out of this summer?" Ethan asked, turning his head to her, his expression earnest.

Riley hesitated. "Honestly? I want adventure, you know? It's my last summer before senior year, and I don't want it to slip by. But I also… I want to have experiences that mean something."

"Experiences that mean something," Ethan echoed. "I get that. I think that's universal—everyone wants to feel something genuine." He looked off into the distance, as if wrapped in his own thoughts. "For me, camp's always been a place to figure out who I am. And with all the creepy stories flying around, I'm kinda curious about the ghost stuff."

Riley's heart raced at the mention of ghosts. Her mind immediately flickered to her encounter with Caleb, the chilly aura that still lingered, the unearthly sorrow etched in his translucent eyes. "You really believe there's something to them?"

"I mean, I don't know," he shrugged, his casual demeanor contrasting with the brewing tempest of emotions in her. "I find the unknown fascinating. It makes life interesting, right? When you dive into the mysteries, you find things about yourself you didn't know existed."

"I guess that makes sense," she replied softly, glancing at him sideways. "But sometimes, I wonder if some things are just better left unexplored, you know? Like, what if you open a door you can't close again?"

Ethan's brow furrowed, a hint of surprise sparkling in his eyes. "You're saying you're afraid of the supernatural?"

"No."

"No? So quick to say that. I guess you really are a ghost wrangler."

They paused, the soft lapping of water against the lakeshore creating a serene backdrop as they stood by the water's edge. The surface shimmered under the light of the stars, reflecting a canvas of twinkling constellations. "I think of it this way: every story has a lesson. Ghosts, legends—maybe they're here to teach us something."

"They usually do." Riley chuckled, but her heart ached at the thought. The weight of her hidden connection to Caleb gnawed at her, a direct contradiction to the warmth she felt next to Ethan.

Against her skin, the air turned cooler, almost teasingly so. Just as she turned back to Ethan, he reached out, his hand brushing against hers in a gentle, almost tentative gesture. The simple touch sent a jolt of electricity coursing through her, igniting something deep within as their eyes locked.

"I really appreciate you, Riley," he confessed, his voice barely above a whisper. The sincerity radiating from him felt palpable, enveloping her like a warm embrace. "It's refreshing to meet someone who thinks like you."

Her breath hitched. In that moment, surrounded by the quiet hum of nature, everything felt magnified—the shadows of the trees, the light dancing on the water, and the tension building between them. She wanted to plunge into the depths of those blue eyes, to understand the secrets and desires swirling beneath the surface.

A shiver trickled down her spine, faint but unmistakable. In that instant, she sensed the chill of another presence hovering just beyond the edges of their connection. The world around her seemed to hesitate—like the calm before a storm. But she fought it, grounding herself in the moment with Ethan.

"I appreciate you, too," Riley said quickly, her heart pounding not just from the coldness creeping in but from a burgeoning affection that threatened to spill over. "Being here with you feels surprisingly… right."

He smiled, a warm and inviting curve of his lips that made Riley melt inside. "Maybe we can make this summer unforgettable—in ways that we never expected."

Their fingers lingered together, as if time had momentarily suspended itself, and they stood at the cusp of something vast and new. The serene reflection of starlight on the lake quietly echoed the yearning between them, a moment shimmering with promise.

But just as the air thickened with unspoken possibilities, a sudden rustling in the trees startled Riley. She pulled her hand away instinctively and turned to scan the shadows beyond. The chill intensified, wrapping around her like a vengeful shroud.

"Did you hear that?" Riley's voice trembled slightly, breaking through the stillness. Anxiety prickled at her skin, her memory racing back to Caleb's sorrowful eyes.

Ethan remained unfazed, chuckling softly. "Probably just a raccoon or something. They're always lurking around. Don't tell me you're scared of little woodland creatures?"

"Not afraid. Just… on edge," she replied defensively, but the uncertainty seeped through. *They always like to make an entrance…*

With a bemused smile, Ethan stepped closer, putting a comforting hand on her shoulder. "I guess we all feel something when faced with the unknown. Fear can make us stronger, too. It's how we cope with what lies behind the veil."

Riley looked up into his eyes, searching for reassurance and a deeper connection. Yet amidst the warmth of their moment, a flicker of ethereal light caught her eye from across the lake, sending her heart racing anew.

whispers from the past

Riley lay on her bed, staring at the wooden beams of the cabin ceiling, replaying the evening like a broken record. Ethan's laughter still echoed in her mind, bright and warm, contrasting sharply with the unsettling chill she felt just before their fingers brushed. How could one moment feel so exhilarating while the next haunted her thoughts? She could still see the surprise in Ethan's piercing blue eyes when she had shared her hesitance toward ghost stories, the way his smile faltered before he quickly masked it with humor.

Her heart raced, caught in the delicious turmoil of youth—a fluttering excitement began to blur the lines between reality and the supernatural. She tucked her knees to her chest, trying to suffocate the thoughts threatening to distract her. Was she really connecting with Ethan, or was it just her imagination fueling the fire ignited by her ghostly encounter with Caleb?

Riley couldn't shake the damn ghost, even after convincing herself it was just some crap her brain conjured up from exhaustion. When she finally closed her eyes to catch some Z's, that eerie chill she'd brushed off earlier crept back, enveloping her like a freaking ghostly blanket. Shit got real intense when she started seeing Caleb's mournful face behind her eyelids.

There was this raw, gut-wrenching pain in his spectral eyes, a loss so deep it threatened to suck her in. Ethan, on the other hand, sparked daydreams that left her feeling all warm and fuzzy. But Caleb? His presence tugged at something darker within her, pulling her into a twisted, intricate maze she wasn't sure she wanted to navigate.

She rolled onto her side, trying to find comfort in the chirping crickets outside. But the rhythmic chorus just made her heart beat faster. *How the hell was she supposed to deal with all this without losing her damn mind?* The weight of everything—her feelings, the weird ghost stuff—it was too much. She felt like she was about to explode.

Hours passed before she drifted into a fitful sleep, the darkness quieted only by the gentle rustling of branches.

She awoke abruptly, feeling a presence close by. A whisper of cold air sailed past her warmth, stirring her from the depths of her dreams. Riley blinked and gasped, eyes wide as she adjusted to the dim light of the moon creeping through the cabin window. Caleb's translucent figure stood before her, more defined than before, shimmering with an urgency that sent shivers racing down her spine.

"Riley," his voice floated through the stillness, echoing softly, a blend of longing and desperation. The sound wrapped around her like mist, both exhilarating and terrifying.

Her heart thrummed in her chest. "Caleb?" she managed to whisper, confusion clouding her thoughts. He appeared even closer than during their last encounter, an ethereal glow illuminating the details of his face marred by sorrow. The intensity in his eyes cut through her uncertainty, making her both uneasy and mesmerized.

"Please… listen," he beckoned, reaching out a hand. It was momentary; just the gesture sent waves of emotion crashing over her. He was pleading, and Riley felt an instinctive need to lean into his pain for reasons she couldn't fully grasp.

Riley sat up straight, the blankets sliding off her shoulders. "What is it? What do you want to tell me?" The question fluttered between them, tinged with hesitation but awash with curiosity.

Caleb's gaze intensified as he focused on her, his presence vibrating with unspoken energy. He stepped closer, shadows curling around him, and he glanced to the side, as though unsure of what lurked beyond her sight.

"You have to know," he whispered, the desolation in his voice slicing through Riley's heart. "It's… about what happened. Camp Willowood—there's danger. I couldn't protect… not then." The pain in his eyes flared, an eternal wound that had never healed, and her breath caught. The weight of his loss coursed through the air, wrapping around them both.

Riley scooted closer to the edge of the bed, entranced by the tortured soul before her. "Danger? What do you mean? Is someone in trouble?"

Caleb shook his head sadly, his translucent form wavering slightly as the shadows shifted. "It's not about them. It's about me. About… the night I was taken." He paused, collecting himself, looking down at the floor as if grappling with something unutterable.

Riley sensed a mix of urgency and fear emanating from him, a force almost palpable against the backdrop of her cabin's darkness. She reached out, her fingers brushing against the edge of the bed. "You need to explain."

His ethereal gaze locked with hers, making her feel exposed yet oddly safe. "I can't leave… until my story is told. The truth, Riley. You're the only one who can see me… find it."

Riley's pulse quickened. The room felt colder, the shadows receding as if retreating from his words. "What happened, Caleb? How can I help you?"

His breath—or what would have been—shuddered in the air, and Caleb shifted, becoming blurred around the edges as if the weight of the past threatened to overwhelm him. "You have to understand… it wasn't just an accident. I need you to uncover what kept me here."

Questions swarmed Riley's mind, pummeling her like a relentless hailstorm. Caught between the damn urgency in Caleb's voice and her screwed-up feelings for Ethan, she was buzzing with the looming ripple effect of her choices.

"Wait," she said, realizing her voice trembled. "You're saying you—"

But before she could finish, Caleb's face shifted, a flash of something dark clouding his features. "Riley, find the diary —the one hidden in the lodge. It holds the key. You've got to act before it's too late." With that, his form began to flicker, wavering as urgency surged through his ghostly essence.

"Caleb, please!" Desperation tinged her plea as he began to dissolve into the moonlight. "What do I do? I need you to…"

"Just believe," he murmured, and then he was gone, leaving the air heavy with unresolved tension and a lingering cold that made her shiver.

Riley collapsed onto her bed, her heartbeat racing out of control. The ghost's words echoed in her mind: she had to know the truth. But how could she reconcile this quest with

"Listen? To what—what do you need?" The words tasted strange on her tongue, a mix of fear and intrigue. The weight of their exchange began to settle over her like a heavy fog.

He moved closer still; the ethereal glow surrounding him illuminated the area, casting flickering shadows along the porch. "The lore. The stories of this place—they're more than fiction. It's all woven together." He hesitated, searching her blue eyes for something. "You don't have to be afraid."

"I'm not afraid," she said, her voice barely above a whisper.

"I wish I could show you," Caleb said, his voice dropping to an intimate hush. "But you have to trust me."

Riley shook her head slowly, the instinct to flee clawing at her. Yet beneath the fear, an undeniable pull coursed through her, urging her to understand, to listen. In that moment, everything else faded—Ethan, the camp, her friends—the universe shrank to just her and the ghost before her, echoing across the barrier of existence.

"If that's what you say," she breathed.

That flicker of playfulness returned to Caleb's features. "I won't bite, I promise."

The air felt electric between them, the world around seemingly suspended. For a heartbeat, she considered the inexplicable pull they shared, the threads that connected her to the emotional connection slowly blossoming with Ethan? The overwhelming duality of conviction and doubt bruised her spirit.

Battling a whirlwind of thoughts, she gazed into the shadowy corners of the room, struggling to steady her breath. Riley understood she needed to take action, yet she felt the weight of the approaching storm of emotions—before it all slipped away like vapor.

* * *

AN UNSETTLING STILLNESS wrapped around Riley as she lay in bed, the silence of the night punctuated only by the distant sounds of crickets. Her heart raced, remnants of her prior conversation with Ethan swimming in her mind, but then, from the shadows, a shiver darted down her spine. Caleb stood before her again, ethereal and translucent, his sorrowful gaze locking onto hers.

His presence felt weighty, and she instinctively pulled her blankets tighter around her shoulders.

Caleb raised a hand, fingers outstretched, his expression a mixture of pleading and gentle encouragement. Riley could see his mouth forming sounds, but no words escaped. It was as if his very essence yearned to spill out, to share the grief and longing muddling up his spectral existence. She watched him, waiting for her heart to stop pitter-pattering against her ribs.

"Caleb," she whispered, hesitant but firm. "What is it?"

He couldn't voice it, but his gaze spoke volumes. The depths of his sorrow told her there was more to his story, layers yet unseen beneath the surface. He gestured toward the cabin window, where the moonlight spilled in, illuminating his form. There was an urgency in his movements, a silent plea that begged her to understand.

Riley followed his gesture hesitantly, feeling a magnetic pull toward him. As she gazed into his sorrowful eyes, images blossomed in her mind—snapshots of laughter, sunlight dancing through the trees, and the rhythm of campers splashing in the swimming hole. It was as if a door had opened wide, revealing the vibrancy of a lifelong extinguished.

She saw Caleb, laughing with a group of friends, their youthful faces alight with pure joy. They ran through the woods, unburdened by the weight of loss, filled only with the exhilaration of summer. She saw bonfire nights filled with stories that curled into the night sky like wisps of smoke, hands raised high for marshmallow toasting, and the warm glow of friendship.

Her heart ached in sympathy, squeezing painfully as images shifted. The carefree laughter faded, replaced by whispers of anguish. Abruptly, the light shifted in the memory, darkening as a storm cloud swept in, twisting the narrative into something sinister. She witnessed Caleb standing alone, looking out over a lake now cast in shadow, isolation swirling fiercely around him, tying knots of despair in his chest. The joy from before was snuffed out, replaced with a devastating melancholy.

Riley's breath quickened as the memory flickered and changed again. A vision of chaos enveloped her—a figure, jealousy evident in their angry demeanor, a spark igniting a sequence of tragic events. A fight erupted, voices layered with betrayal, and then a loss that cut deeply through the camp like an icy gust of wind.

"Caleb!" she gasped, her hands trembling as the weight of his unspoken history crashed against her mind, consuming her senses.

He turned toward her, a look of longing in his tortured expression. In that moment, Riley felt everything. The heaviness of his regrets, the guilt that tightened around his chest, and an endless thirst for closure. He gestured again, this time towards the sounds of the camp—the rustling leaves, the tired laughter of campers winding down from the day's activities; they were worlds apart, he and they.

"Can't you let go?" Her voice trembled, the words heavy in the air as they lodged deep in her throat. She faltered, meeting his gaze again. "Why are you still here?"

Caleb's gaze didn't waver, and she felt drawn to him, compulsion clawing at her heart. He moved slightly closer, his presence invoking a sense of warmth despite the spectral chill in the air. As she focused on the haunting look in his eyes, the answer curled around her thoughts—he was tethered to the past, unable to break free from the pain that bound him to Camp Willowood.

Riley's pulse raced, overwhelmed by empathy. "You're trapped, aren't you?"

He nodded slowly, and the ache in her chest intensified, fueled by the weight of his untold story. She felt a connection to his unresolved pain. There was a longing, a need for understanding that craved space in her heart. Suddenly, the chilling tales of Camp Willowood felt trivial compared to the life Caleb once lived, the tragedy that led him to this moment.

The visions pressed forward. She saw more of his life—the mundane moments of sun-drenched days spent caring for campers.

"What happened to you?" she asked quietly, not expecting a reply, just a release of her own curiosity and sorrow.

Caleb's eyes glistened with unshed tears, this spectral existence unable to fully express the emotions that rippled beneath the surface. The memories stirred again, and more images surged forth—a broken promise, scornful whispers among friends, and a moment of bravery gone tragically wrong. He reached out toward her, fingers barely brushing against the air, a silent invitation echoing in the void.

Riley swallowed hard as the weight of empathy settled over her like a heavy quilt. She wanted to unravel this mystery, to understand not just the horror of his death, but the vibrancy of his life before it was taken. "I'll help you."

In response, he stepped back, and though the distance between them hardly shifted, it felt monumental. Caleb's form flickered, revealing the depth of the sorrow within him, before collapsing into the shadowy room behind him, refusing to let go of the connection while keeping his emotional barrier intact.

As the heaviness subsided, determination gripped Riley, forcing her to confront the gravity of what lay ahead. She understood now that Caleb's story was intricately tied to hers, a web bound by unreleased fears and hidden truths merely waiting for someone brave enough to pry them open.

She made a silent promise to him and to herself—she would learn everything about Caleb's life, and unravel the tragedy that bound him to the camp. She would dive into its history, past the campfire tales, and uncover the real story that lingered in the whispers of the trees and the stillness of the lake.

Caleb flickered a final time, his eyes locking onto hers with a twin mixture of sorrow and gratitude. And then he faded, leaving only the haunting echo of his longing for release lingering in the air.

Alone in her cabin, Riley burned with an unfaltering need to discover the truth.

* * *

RILEY RUBBED the sleep from her eyes, the memories of Caleb's visit still vivid in her mind. The morning sun poured through the cabin window, casting a golden glow across the wooden floors. Her heart raced; the urge to uncover Caleb's story consumed her. Just outside her cabin, laughter and the rustling of eager campers gathered for breakfast filled the air.

After breakfast, with her determination bubbling over, Riley cornered her cabinmates near the activity board.

"Guys, I need your help." Her voice spilled over the chatter as she gestured to them.

Maya, a girl with bright pink hair and an adventurous spirit, leaned in with a grin. "What's up, Riley? You've got that look in your eyes—like you've just found another ghost book!"

"It's about Caleb," Riley said, excitement electrifying her words. "The ghost I told you about. I want to find out what happened to him. I think he's trying to communicate something important."

Kurt, her cabinmate with skepticism written all over his face, rolled his eyes. "You mean the ghost you dreamt about? Come on, Riley. Ghosts aren't real."

"Yeah, but think about it! He was a camp counselor, and

there's all this history here," she insisted, her intensity unyielding. "I'm convinced there's something—"

"Like a hidden treasure?" Maya chuckled, bumping Riley's shoulder playfully.

"Or a curse!" whispered Jenna, her wide brown eyes sparkling with fright. "What if he's, like, a warning?"

"Let's figure it out," Riley said, shaking off the teasing. "Meet me at the library in an hour. I'll show you what I found."

With a collective nod, her friends agreed, some more eagerly than others. Riley felt the adrenaline surge within; it wasn't just about Caleb anymore—she wanted to dig into the essence of Camp Willowood.

The library was tucked away, a cozy structure made of old timber that smelled faintly of musty books and pine. Its walls held stories of campers long gone, whispering secrets of the past. Sunlight streamed through the tall windows, illuminating the swirl of dust in the air.

Riley scanned the rows of ancient books and narrow shelves, heart racing. Maya's voice cut through her thoughts. "So, where do we start? Don't tell me you brought your ghost-hunting gear."

"Just the spirit of inquiry," Riley replied, winking back with a grin.

Jenna crowded close, her curiosity bubbling. "What am I looking for?"

"I don't know. I just know there's something about him I need to understand," Riley said, her focus shifting to the rows of dusty records. She motioned for her friends to search the stacks while she headed toward a corner that held newspaper clippings.

They rummaged through books and journals filled with fading stories, laughter punctuating their casual investigation. Kurt sat back against a shelf, arms crossed, shaking his head. "You guys really think you're going to uncover some mystery?"

"Just wait and see," Maya replied, tossing a slim volume to the ground. "There's gotta be something in here."

As they continued to explore, the air around Riley felt charged with unearthing secrets. With every flipping page, her excitement grew. The mingling scents of old paper and wood were intoxicating, fueling her determination.

Time slipped away as they dug deeper, scattering papers under the weight of Riley's churning thoughts. She flipped through old camper journals filled with doodles and clumsy handwriting.

"Hey, what do you think Caleb was like?" Maya asked, glancing up. "Was he, like, super serious or fun? Did he have a crush?"

"Wouldn't you want to talk to him before deciding?" Kurt interjected, smirking but curiosity lurking in his voice.

As if the vibe shifted, Riley felt that electric sensation again, the kind that tingled at the back of her neck. She forced herself to focus.

"Okay, I'm looking in the clippings section," she announced, rifling through the brittle pages, and combing through each article with anticipation.

"Look at this!" Jenna shouted, waving a thin paper in front of the group, her voice high with excitement.

"Ugh, what now?" Kurt sighed, standing and moving closer.

Jenna turned the paper toward him, her eyes wide. "It's a newspaper article! It's dated 1975."

Riley's heart raced as she stepped closer. The headline screamed "Tragic Disappearance at Camp Willowood."

A chill washed over her, and she leaned in, scanning the article. "Listen to this," she whispered, her voice trembling slightly.

"It was July 7, 1975, when a camp counselor vanished under suspicious circumstances. Despite extensive searches, no trace of him was found, leaving unresolved questions and grief among staff and campers. Rumors spread that the camp was cursed, a veil of mist lingering where he was last seen."

Riley's eyes widened. "This has to be about Caleb! This has to be…!" She trailed off, her thoughts tangled in a whirlwind of emotion.

"What's the name?" Maya asked, leaning over to catch a glimpse.

"Caleb Whitaker," Riley read aloud, her breath hitching.

Silence enveloped the room as they absorbed the weight of the revelation, each processing the gravity that brushed against their skin. The disbelief simmered in the air.

"Okay, wait a second," Kurt finally said, the smirk wiped from his face. "Are you saying this is *your* ghost?"

"Why else would he keep showing up?" Riley replied, a tremor of excitement threading through her words. "This is why he's haunting the camp! He has unfinished business."

"That's wild," Jenna murmured, her gaze sweeping over the faded words, as if they could feel the echoes of the past in the room.

Maya leaned closer, hands on her knees. "But if he disappeared, how did he die?"

"Maybe he—" Kurt began, but his voice faltered as he tried to piece together the scenario swirling in their minds.

"We have to dig deeper," Riley insisted, heart pounding with purpose. She felt a fire ignite within her. "I need to find out what really happened to Caleb—there should be a diary somewhere."

"A diary?" Jenna asked, "Why the heck didn't you say that before?"

Riley shrugged her shoulders.

A mixture of excitement and trepidation filled the room. The search had taken a significant turn, awakening a drive to uncover the truth hidden within hours of dusty records and forgotten memories.

6
secrets of camp willowood

The library at Camp Willowood felt like a mix of shadows and secrets, its dusty wooden shelves sagging under the burden of stories long neglected. Sunlight poured through slim windows, spilling golden beams onto the faded papers scattered across the tables. Riley was in the center, flanked by her cabinmates: Mia, Jenna, and Alex. The air hummed with a mix of excitement and a touch of anxiety, like the charged moment just before a ghost story kicked off.

"Who knew libraries could be so… eerie?" Mia quipped, brushing dust off an old manual before flipping it open.

"Eerie is definitely an understatement," Riley replied, her voice low as she leaned closer to a tattered logbook. "But I feel like we'll find something huge in here. I can just tell."

"Bring on the ghost tales. I'm ready," Alex said, his eyes sparkling with mischief. He grabbed an old flashlight from the table, waving it playfully like a prop from a horror movie. "Let's shed some light on the secrets buried in this place."

The group's laughter echoed softly, mingling with the scent of old paper and faded ink. As they browsed through decades-old camp manuals and yearbooks, they uncovered a treasure trove of camp history. They shared stories about colorful mishaps during activities and ridiculous pranks played on counselors that only served to strengthen their bond.

"Look at this! 'The Great Marshmallow War of '93!'" Jenna exclaimed, showing them a picture of campers covered in sticky goo. The group erupted in laughter, momentarily forgetting why they were there.

Yet as the mood lightened, it didn't take long for the atmosphere to shift.

Riley found it.

Riley found the journal.

Riley's fingers brushed against an entry in the journal, a passage that sent a chill down her spine, sobering the conversation.

"Hey, listen to this," Riley said, her heart racing a little as she cleared her throat. "This is from the summer of 1975 when a counselor went missing." She read on, her voice lowering.

"It says here,

'The camp was buzzing with rumors of jealousy between counselors. Tensions ran high, particularly surrounding Caleb and his close friend, Jake. Some said it was jealousy over their campsite popularity that led to a dark incident beneath the surface of Camp Willowood.'"

The room fell silent, the laughter replaced by an uneasy tension.

"What does that mean? Dark incident?" Mia questioned, her brows knitted together.

Riley felt a flutter of apprehension in her stomach. "It sounds like there were some serious issues at play," she said, voice barely above a whisper. "It's almost like a backdrop for tragedy."

"I mean, every camp has its drama. It could just be gossip, you know?" Alex shrugged, but his tone defended.

Jenna cut in, her expression pensive. "But it's like, there was more to Caleb than just being a popular dude, you know?

He had his fair share of haters too. Maybe those bad vibes escalated into something serious?"

Riley's attention drifted to another entry, her fingers skimming over the crinkled page.

"Listen to this one:

> 'Caleb never returned from a midnight adventure one night, and searches turned up nothing. Only whispers of a fight between him and Jake surfaced in the days after. The camp closed for an extended period after that summer, the darkness lingering over what transpired.'"

"Wow, someone really needs to make a horror movie out of this," Alex chimed in, but Riley shot him a disapproving glance.

"This isn't funny," she said. "This was someone's life. Caleb deserves the truth."

Mia leaned closer, flipping through the pages with newfound urgency. "We should keep looking for answers. There has to be something more here about Caleb, or even Jake—maybe even why Caleb was targeted."

One entry caught Jenna's attention. "Hey, here's a picture!" She held up a faded photograph of a group of counselors, all sun-kissed and smiling, 1970s attire and hair, their carefree faces beaming at the camera. Caleb stood among them, his smile wide and carefree, barely hinting at the tragedy awaiting him. "Which one is Caleb?"

Riley grabbed the old photograph. She scanned through the group and her eyes halted on one counselor in particular, Caleb. He looked happy, he had a nice smile and he was cute—probably even hot back then—with his long comb-over and poncho. "This is him," she finally said, as the girls all leaned in to take a peek.

"Oh, he's cute," Mia remarked.

"Yeah, wow, what a hottie," Jenna chimed in.

"Do you think Jake is in this photo?" Mia asked, scanning the faces. "They could have been friends back then."

As Riley peered at the photograph, she felt a familiar wave of emotion wash over her, the burdens of Caleb's untold story weighing heavily on her heart. "There's so much we don't know," she murmured, almost to herself. "What if Caleb and Jake had a fallout?"

"I mean, jealousy can lead people to do crazy things," Mia added, shuffling closer to Riley and squinting at the picture. "Look at Caleb. He seems so carefree, so happy. It's unreal to think it could end so tragically. I want to know what happened to him."

"That's it! We need to find Jake's story, too," Riley declared, apprehension about the unknown mingling with determination. "If we can track down what went wrong, maybe we can find closure for Caleb's spirit. It might be the key to understanding why he's stuck here."

With renewed energy, they delved further into the library's secrets. Time slipped away like grains of sand, their focus unyielding as they turned pages and explored every angle of Caleb's story. Each finding heightened Riley's resolve, spurring her on despite the chilling undercurrents threading through their research.

Hours passed, and then Mia's voice rang out once more. "Guys, check this out! Another clipping—this one says that Jake left Camp Willowood immediately after that summer."

Riley's pulse quickened. "Do you think he could still be alive? We could search him out and hear his side of the story."

"Damn, that's a gamble," Jenna said, twirling her hair around her finger as she furrowed her brow. "What if this Jake dude ain't feeling chatty about old times?"

"Or what if he's not ready to face what he did?" Alex added, crossing his arms. "Sounds messy."

Riley's heart raced as she sat back, contemplating all that they had uncovered. Would the truth bring them peace, or would it open old wounds? She sensed that the deeper they probed into this history, the closer she drew to Caleb's world and the questions that swirled around it.

"Half the fun of investigating is the unknown," Riley smiled, her eyes sparkling with determination. "We can't let fear hold us back now. I need to know more about Caleb—and you guys are the best partners I could ask for."

The bonds of their friendship felt stronger, a radiant circle of support encouraging them to confront the mysteries intertwining their lives and the past. As they continued searching through papers and photos, their laughter returned, creating a blend of levity amid the weight of their discoveries. Each page unearthed deepened not only their intrigue about Camp Willowood but also the connections they shared with each other, especially with the ghost calling out for understanding just beyond their grasp.

* * *

IN THE DIMLY LIT LIBRARY OF Camp Willowood, Riley and her friends had created a makeshift research hub. Dust motes danced in the shafts of sunlight filtering through the tall windows, illuminating their eager faces as they surrounded a table piled high with old books, journals, and newspapers. The musty smell of paper clung to them, mixing with the warm scent of pine wafting in from outside.

Riley leaned over the faded 1970s journal, her heart racing as she flipped through the pages. She had been excited since the moment she found the first clue about Caleb's disappearance, but the more she read, the more the whispers of doubt began to creep in from her friends seated nearby.

"I dunno," Jenna said, breaking the silence. "I can't believe I'm doing all this because of a so-called ghost. I mean, come on, Riley. Ghosts? An actual ghost?" Jenna scoffed, rolling her eyes as she tossed papers aside. "You're really buying into these stories?"

"I mean, c'mon, Riley," Tom piped up, his voice dripping with disbelief. "You seriously buyin' this crap about some dude bein' a ghost? Like he's been haunting this camp forever or somethin'?" He shook his head, a smirk playing at the corners of his mouth. "I dunno, man. Sounds like bull to me."

Riley straightened up, frustration bubbling beneath the surface. "But I've seen him—and he's real! He showed me flashes of his life here, moments that matter. You guys don't get it!"

"Maybe you just got freaked out in the dark and imagined it," Jenna countered, raising an eyebrow doubtfully.

Riley's hands clenched into fists. She took a deep breath, trying to calm the storm brewing inside her. "I can't explain it to you; you just have to trust me. There's something important about him, and I won't let you dismiss it."

She glanced over at Ethan, who had suddenly appeared in the doorway, his blue eyes searching hers as though he weighed her words. A flicker of understanding passed between them, and he stood. "Listen, guys. I've seen things I couldn't explain too. Weird things happen here all the time. Just because you haven't seen it doesn't mean it isn't real."

"Exactly," Riley's voice gained strength, turning back to her friends. "I'm not here just to indulge in ghost stories; I'm trying to uncover a truth that deserves to be told."

Jenna leaned back, crossing her arms. "Okay, but what if you're just chasing shadows? What if you're wasting your time?"

"Then it's my time to waste," she shot back, a hint of defiance racing through her.

Tom threw his hands up, a sarcastic grin spreading across his face. "Alright, alright, I hear ya. But c'mon, we can't just go poking around in the past like it's some treasure hunt. What the hell are we supposed to find?"

Jenna cocked her head, arms folded tightly across her chest. "Yeah, but what if you're just running after ghosts? You might be spinning your wheels for nothing."

Riley's defiance flashed in her eyes. "Then it's my time to burn. But I'm not gonna stop until I find the truth."

Tom let out an exaggerated sigh, a smirk tugging at his lips. "Fine, fine. Just don't go dragging us down some damn rabbit hole, alright?"

Riley's brow furrowed, and she returned to the journal, her fingers trailing over passages about Camp Willowood's history. She stumbled upon an entry detailing Caleb's close relationship with Jacob.

"Wait…" she announced. Her voice pulled the group's attention back as if a spell had been cast. "Look at this. Caleb was really close with this Jacob guy. They were practically inseparable."

Ethan moved closer, leaning over her shoulder to read the journal's worn pages. "What does it say?"

"They talked about how Caleb looked up to Jacob, how he was like a mentor," Riley explained. "He encouraged him as a counselor, and there are mentions of something going wrong between them—tensions, jealousy. I think this might be tied to Caleb's death."

Tom shifted uncomfortably, caught off guard by the weight of her discovery. "So…what now? You think jealousy led to his disappearance?"

Riley nodded fervently, determination swirling within her. "It could be. If Jacob had some influence over Caleb, something might've driven them apart. Maybe it was stronger than just a friendship."

"Or just some camp drama," Jenna muttered, flipping her own journal closed.

"I don't know about that," Ethan interjected, his voice calm yet insistent. "The kind of drama that happens in a place like this can spiral. All it takes is one bad moment. All I'm saying is that we shouldn't rule out the possibility."

Riley met Ethan's gaze. He believed in her. A rush of gratitude flowed through her as he placed a supportive hand on her shoulder.

"But how do we find out more?" Tom asked, his earlier bravado wavering. "Do we just ask ghosts?"

Riley felt the corner of her mouth twitch upwards despite the tension. "Actually, I think we should search outside the library, maybe try to find clues around the campgrounds. Explore where Caleb spent his time, where he might have had issues with Jacob."

"Sounds risky," Jenna said warily.

"Maybe not," Ethan suggested. "The camp's full of old stories. If there's any physical evidence left behind, we might find something that connects Caleb to Jacob. Plus, people are always drawn to the stories in the shared spaces—places like the old cabins or the dock."

"Whoa, hold up," Tom said, raising his hands defensively. "You want us to snoop around? I don't know, it sounds way too much like a horror movie trope to me."

"I'm game," Jenna said, surprising everyone. "As long as we stick together."

Riley felt a flicker of relief wash over her. If Jenna was on board, perhaps Tom could be persuaded too. "Let's just look for something that leads to Caleb's truth. It'll be fun! We'll make it a part of our camp adventure."

"We can start at the cabins," Ethan suggested, his voice holding a confident edge. "I can show you the places you might not have seen yet. I've been around long enough to know where the old secrets linger."

Riley's excitement grew with each passing moment. "Really? You'll help?"

"Of course," he replied with a grin, the warmth in his voice sending an electric jolt through her. "I wouldn't let you do this alone."

Jenna shot Tom a teasing smirk. "Looks like it's settled then. Let's go uncover some camp mysteries."

With her friends finally rallying around her, despite the tension, Riley felt a surge of determination rising within her. They replaced the research materials, hastily stuffing journals and clippings into their bags with the thrill of an impending adventure.

As they made their way to the door, a wave of exhilaration swept over Riley, and she realized they were embarking on a search for more than just answers. It was a journey to validate Caleb's existence, to understand a past that remained hauntingly elusive. All while navigating her own budding feelings for Ethan, whose presence kept pulsating like an anchor in her chaotic heart.

* * *

THE WARM AFTERNOON sun filtered through the canopy of trees as Riley, her friends, and Ethan set off on their exploratory adventure. Armed with a sense of determination and a thirst for answers, they made their way toward the cluster of cabins that had once housed the counselors during Caleb's time at Camp Willowood.

Riley led the way, her heart pounding with a mix of trepidation and excitement. As they approached Caleb's former cabin, the overgrown vines and forgotten memorials painted a picture of neglect, as if time itself had turned a blind eye to the echoes of the past.

"This is it," she whispered, her fingers tracing the weathered wood of the cabin's exterior. A strange sense of familiarity washed over her, as if she could almost feel Caleb's presence lingering in the air.

Ethan stepped forward, gently pushing aside the vines that obscured the doorway. "Let's see what we can find."

The group ventured inside, their footsteps echoing through the dusty interior. Riley's eyes scanned the room, taking in every detail — the faded photographs on the walls, the remnants of personal belongings left behind, and a tattered journal peeking out from beneath a worn mattress.

With trembling hands, she reached for a journal, her fingertips brushing against the frayed leather cover. As she opened the pages, Caleb's elegantly scrawled handwriting came into view, revealing glimpses of his youthful aspirations and dreams.

"He wanted to be a teacher," Riley murmured, her voice laced with awe and sadness. "He loved working with kids and sharing his passion for the outdoors."

As she read further, the words seemed to leap off the page, transporting her back in time. She could almost picture Caleb sitting at the desk, pen in hand, pouring his heart onto the pages as the sounds of laughter and campfire songs drifted through the open window.

A sudden chill swept through the cabin, causing the others to shiver and draw closer together. Riley's breath caught in her throat as Caleb's ghostly form materialized beside her, his expression a haunting mix of pain and gratitude.

Their eyes locked, and in that moment, Riley felt an inexplicable connection – a bridge between the past and present, spanning decades of unanswered questions and unresolved grief. She could sense Caleb's appreciation for her efforts, his gratitude that someone was finally listening to the story he had longed to tell.

As she clutched the diary to her chest, Riley's determination solidified. She knew, without a doubt, that she was on the right path – a path that would lead her to uncover the truth about Caleb's fate and bring him the justice he deserved.

With Caleb's spectral presence lingering beside her, she turned to face her friends, her eyes alight with a newfound sense of purpose. "We're not going to stop until we find out what happened to him," she declared, her voice unwavering. "Caleb deserves to have his story told, and we're going to be the ones to do it."

7

torn connections

Riley strolled along the worn path toward the dining hall, the chatter of her friends creating a vibrant backdrop as they relished the mid-afternoon sun. The smell of grilled burgers wafted in the air, mingling with the sweet scent of wildflowers lining the edge of the camp. Yet, despite the festive atmosphere, an uneasy weight rested in her chest. Each step felt like she was trudging through mud, the excitement of her recent discoveries about Caleb fading like the echoes of laughter behind her.

Inside the dining hall, sunlight streamed through the large windows, illuminating the long tables filled with campers. Riley grabbed a tray, her mind wandering to the lessons Caleb had shown her the day before. Each fleeting moment with him peeled back layers of the camp's hidden history, but with every revelation came a pang of guilt. She wanted to dive into the depths of Caleb's story, to unearth the truth about his tragic past, yet there was Ethan, with his easy charm and warm smile, waiting for her to engage.

"Hey, Earth to Riley!" Ethan waved a hand in front of her face, the infectious grin never leaving his lips. His sandy hair glinted in the sunlight as he leaned closer. "You just zoned out on me."

Riley snapped back to reality, her heart racing. "Sorry. Just... thinking about today's activities. You know how it is with cabin chores." She forced a laugh, the sound feeling hollow even to her ears.

"Right," Ethan replied, taking a seat across from her, his brows now knitting together with concern. "Everything okay? You seem a little... I don't know, distant." A hint of disappointment washed over his features, shadows creeping alongside the light.

"Just... got a lot on my mind," she said, shoving a fry into her mouth, trying to cloak the turmoil swirling within. She had just shared part of Caleb's story with her friends, and yet here she was, sitting in front of the one person who radiated possibility, and all she could think about was the ghost who wasn't even alive.

"Are you sure that's all it is?" Ethan leaned back in his chair, crossing his arms. His piercing blue eyes bore into her. The tension soldered between them like a tight wire stretching dangerously thin. "I mean, you've been acting a little off since we've started hanging out. If something's bothering you…"

"No, really. I'm fine." The words came out quicker than she intended, making her feel defensive. She could see the small flicker of hurt behind Ethan's expression, the way his smile faltered just a notch, forcing her heart to clench.

"But, like, Riley, if you're not having fun at camp… you're not just here to help me with the s'mores and ghost stories, right?"

"Of course," she said, her voice tinged with a nervous tremor. "I'm having a blast! It's just… a lot. You know?"

"Right." He nodded slowly, each word feeling wrapped in confusion. "So, tell me then. What are you thinking about? Summer plans? Me?" He smirked to ease the tension, flipping it into a playful challenge, but the light faded away like the sun slipping behind a cloud.

"All of the above," she said, attempting to lift her spirits with a smile, though it felt more like a mask. The truth weighed heavily between them. Ethan's energy was both thrilling and reassuring, yet Caleb lingered in the back of her mind, his whisper echoing like a distant siren's call.

Riley diverted her gaze to the table, focusing on her food, on the way her fingers fidgeted with the napkin. The scrutiny in Ethan's eyes felt unbearable. He was nothing less than charming, the kind of guy she had always imagined to swirl into her daydreams. Yet, as Caleb's haunting visage seeped into her mind, she felt the divide grow heavier, stretching farther than she could reconcile.

"What's the story with you and this ghost, anyway?" Ethan's tone shifted to one of teasing once more, but there was a hint of something deeper underlying his words. "If you're not careful, you'll be caught in some whirlwind romance with a guy who can't even hold hands."

"I told you, it's just stories. I heard some spooky stuff around the camp, that's all." She brushed it aside, feeling defensive again, embarrassed. She didn't want to let the magic of her evenings with Caleb taint this lively new friendship. Yet, honesty tumbled within her like tangled autumn leaves.

"You know," he said, a soft chuckle escaping him, "you're a bit of an enigma, Riley Parker. One second, you're diving into ghost lore, and the next, you're right here with me. I don't get how you pack so much in that pretty little head of yours."

The compliment brought a flush of warmth to her cheeks, but before she could respond, a shrill laugh erupted from the table nearby. It sliced through the air, awakening Riley from the spell of her internal conflict.

Riley turned in their direction, trying to ground herself in the moment. Camp laughter rang around the hall, and the air buzzed with a light-infused joy that felt just out of reach. She daydreamed about having fun with Ethan, a carefree summer spent running through the woods, a world free of ghosts and tragedy. Yet, Caleb's unbreakable bond, his silent plea for help, hung like an anchor, tying her to something darker.

"Riley?" Ethan interrupted her reverie, tilting his head. His expression hinted at confusion. "Seriously. Are you alright? Because I feel like I'm talking to a wall here."

His concern shone like a spotlight, illuminating the distance she had started to grow. "I just… I'm still trying to adjust to all of this. Camp life, life at home, my friends. It's a lot. I thought I'd better have it all figured out by now." She let her breath out, freed from the tight grip of guilt just for a moment, far from the repercussions of her attraction to both him and Caleb.

He nodded, clearly searching for a way forward. "I get it. But just know, we all have our things to deal with. If you ever want to talk about yours, I'm here."

Appreciation bloomed in her chest at his sincerity, but it quickly morphed into confusion. How could she explain Caleb to Ethan, someone who radiated warmth but didn't belong in her supernatural world?

"I know that," she finally said, her tone softer. "Thanks, Ethan. I appreciate that." She could feel a rush of affection building, but in that same moment, Caleb's image flickered in her mind, causing her a sense of fracture.

"Just don't disappear on me," Ethan's grin reappeared, but the laughter in his eyes couldn't conceal how he read her inner struggle.

With a forced smile, Riley engaged in conversation, trying to push the layers of distance down. She laughed when needed, shared in the light banter, eager to dispel the tension relaxing between them. But inside, the battle raged on. Her connection to Caleb tugged at her heart, the ghostly allure blurring the line she needed to draw.

Her thoughts drifted between life and death, laughter and longing, one foot anchored to this reality and the other toeing the edge of something otherworldly. As the afternoon sun continued to drench the camp in gold, Riley knew she faced a choice — to embrace the warmth of living connections or to delve further into the depth of the unknown.

* * *

THE NIGHT AIR shimmered with starlight as campers gathered around a flickering bonfire, their laughter and chatter rising like smoke into the canopy of trees above. The crackling flames cast silhouettes against the wooden cabins, creating an enchanting yet eerie backdrop. S'mores melted over the heat, filling the air with the sweet scent of chocolate and toasted marshmallows.

Riley snuggled into her sweatshirt, feeling the warmth seep into her skin. As she settled onto a log beside her cabinmates, she stole a glance at Ethan, who effortlessly commanded the attention of the group. His sandy hair glowed in the firelight, and his piercing blue eyes sparkled with enthusiasm.

"Alright, everyone," Ethan began, flashing a mischievous grin that sent warmth flooding through Riley's chest. "Tonight, we're going to turn the ghost story tradition on its head! I want you all to create your own ghostly tales inspired by events here at Camp Willowood."

Riley's heart quickened at the challenge. She loved weaving stories, but a delicate tremor of anxiety twisted in her stomach. Inspiration struck her, but the looming thought of Caleb loomed heavier than any ghost story. The connection she felt with him was indefinable—an emotion that both excited and terrified her.

"First rule: it has to have an element of truth," Ethan continued, pacing a bit as he gestured animatedly. "Camp legends, historical events, even creepy things you've heard from staff or other campers. Let's see how creative you can get!"

Laughter erupted, and Riley's cabinmates began whispering excitedly among themselves, exchanging ideas and brainstorming. But all Riley could think about was the chilling presence of Caleb and how deeply his story connected to the fabric of Camp Willowood.

As the campers took turns sharing snippets of their fabricated tales, Riley's heart raced. The firelight flickered, casting dancing shadows across their eager faces.

"And then," one camper declared, "the ghost of a vengeful counselor stalks the woods, whispering secrets to those who venture too close."

Riley's mind drifted, her heart tugging at the edges of her consciousness. The mention of a counselor jolted her thoughts to Caleb, who had become both her inspiration and her distraction. *Was it selfish to weave his story into hers?* He had been trapped, longing for a connection, and here she was, caught between two worlds, yearning for two different souls.

After a few more stories, Ethan nodded toward her. "Riley! Why don't you give it a shot?"

Everyone turned to her, and the attention felt suffocating. Her chest tightened as she sought to find the right words but found only Caleb's haunted visage staring back at her. Each blink recalled his aching eyes and the longing etched on his translucent face.

"I'm not… I'm not sure I can come up with anything," she said, forcing a smile that felt brittle.

She noticed Ethan's brow crease, a hint of concern flickering across his features. "C'mon, Riley! You're the expert on ghost stories. Plus, we're all friends here. Just think of something that speaks to you."

Riley hesitated, torn between the warmth radiating from Ethan and the cold pull that beckoned from the shadows. Her thoughts drifted to an image of Caleb, hovering just out of reach, his ethereal form caught in a frozen moment, desperate for resolution.

"What if," she began, her voice slightly wavering as she focused on Ethan, "what if you found an old journal belonging to a counselor who disappeared? Yeah, and the entries seemed normal at first but started to get darker, filled with sinister sketches and cryptic warnings?"

As she wove her narrative, the fire crackled, capturing the campers' attention as they leaned in closer, mesmerized by her voice.

"Over time, the counselor was driven mad by whispers in the woods, believing other counselors were conspiring against him. He wrote about seeing figures in the trees, shadows moving, and the feeling of being watched."

The fire flickered ominously, and as she continued, her gaze drifted to the periphery. There, in the shadows, Caleb hovered with an almost childlike curiosity. He was watching her, his expression a mix of sadness and understanding.

A thrill pulsed through her veins, igniting memories of their connection. She faltered, her story growing heavy with the weight of her emotions as she pronounced the final frame. "But in the end, the counselor vanished—leaving nothing behind but his journal. Some say he became a part of the forest, forever lost… and the whispers still linger, looking for someone who can hear."

The campfire crackled louder, and a collective intake of breath punctuated her tale. Her friends cheered and clapped, excitement dancing in their eyes.

Ethan beamed at her, pride written across his handsome features. "That was awesome, Riley! You've totally captured the essence of the camp."

She felt a flush of warmth at his compliment, but her heart still beat for Caleb, echoing the desire for a connection that felt almost forbidden.

As the storytelling continued, the atmosphere shifted, growing palpable with anticipation. Campers exchanged wild plots, some gruesome, some hilariously absurd. But in the backdrop, Caleb remained, his presence ever so close, drawing her gaze. It was thrilling and terrifying, an insistent tension threading through her.

Suddenly, one of the campers spoke about a specific incident where a counselor was found wandering in the woods, unable to remember how they'd gotten there. For a second, Riley thought it might've been Caleb, but she shook the thought away.

"Oh!" a camper shouted, "What if the jumps from dimension to dimension made it so one counselor can't leave? They're trapped between this world and the next!"

Riley's stomach knotted. The camper's wild imagination seemed to mirror her thoughts, spiraling into a reality she couldn't fully grasp. Caleb had entered her life unexpectedly, alive with emotions yet undeniably tied to the supernatural.

The fire popped, and she could feel Caleb's longing weight in the air. The distance between her and the living world felt insurmountable. She fought against the swirl of emotions; guilt for having uncovered his story mixed with the happiness Ethan brought her.

Midway through someone else's story, Riley got caught up staring at Caleb, unsure of what to make of the longing in his ethereal eyes. He mirrored her own confusion. Just then, she felt a strong, soft chill brush against her skin, wrapping around her in an embrace that made her heartache.

"Riley, you good?" Ethan broke into her thoughts, concern lacing his gentle tone.

"Yeah," she replied, forcing a smile. "Just… lost in thought for a second."

He nodded and continued to engage with their friends, leaving her to grapple with the whirlwind of emotions. A part of her was tethered to the laughter and warmth of the campfire, while another part yearned for an understanding that only Caleb could provide.

As the night wore on, the group weaved tales of the dark and dreary, shadows playing against their animated faces. Clapping and laughter echoed, yet in the shadows, Riley felt an unbreakable bond to the ghost whose presence turned her heart into a battlefield. The lingering question echoed in the depths of her thoughts: How would she navigate this supernatural tangle of hope and despair, love and loss, without losing herself entirely?

AS THE CRACKLING campfire faded behind them, the laughter and chatter of their fellow campers drifted into the night, leaving Riley and Ethan in an unsettling silence. The shadows of the towering trees stretched across the pathway, and Riley could feel the cool night air settling around her like a shroud. She walked a few steps behind Ethan, eyeing the way his athletic form moved smoothly, his sandy hair tousled yet still perfect under the stars. She felt a sense of disconnect growing heavier with each passing moment.

"Riley?" Ethan turned abruptly, his gaze piercing and earnest against the backdrop of flickering starlight.

Riley stopped, her heart racing. The concern etched on his face made her stomach turn. "Yeah?"

"You're acting weird. Preoccupied," he said, crossing his arms, a gesture that only made him appear more serious. "What's going on? Any new developments with the ghost?"

Riley's breath caught in her throat. The words she had been wrestling with all evening flickered at the edge of her mind.

It felt like a secret too delicate to share. But there was a part of her that craved honesty—the kind that could fracture her heart into a million pieces all at once.

"Ethan, it's just—"

He stepped closer, his blue eyes narrowing slightly. "Just what? You've been pulling away, and I need to know if I'm imagining it. Do I have a chance here?"

Riley felt the tightness in her chest constricting further. She wanted to reach out, to assure him that it wasn't him. That he was everything she had come to admire and crave during her time at Camp Willowood, but how could she explain a bond with someone who existed solely in another realm?

The words tumbled out of her, the compulsion to reveal her truth overwhelming. "I've been thinking a lot about the journal," She added quickly.

Ethan's brows furrowed as shock settled in. "What about it? Anything new?"

"No. Just a lot of questions."

"Insane," he cut in, his voice sharp and incredulous, an edge of disbelief brushing the surface.

Riley's heart sank. The warmth she had once felt between them dimmed, replaced by an icy touch of his skepticism. "I'm sorry Ethan, I'm sorry I'm not good company."

"Have you seen the ghost again?" Ethan asked, still skeptical.

"I see him every day," Riley admitted, sad.

"You're saying you actually see him every day?" He shook his head, backing away slightly as though he had just stumbled upon an unholy sight. "Riley, that's not... that's just not possible."

"I know it sounds crazy, but—"

"And, what does he do? Does he talk to you? Do you have a conversation?"

Riley stopped walking and gazed over at the trees. "Yes, we have a conversation."

Ethan couldn't believe what he was hearing. "Why?"

"Because," she breathed, feeling her throat tighten as a rush of emotion surged inside. "Caleb... he's lonely. He's stuck and needs help finding peace. I can feel it, Ethan." Her voice softened. "I can feel his pain. I just can't walk away from that."

The silence that fell between them was suffocating, filled with the weight of unspoken truths. Ethan's expression shifted from disbelief to something deeper, something vulnerable. "So, that's it? You want to help this ghost instead of being here, with me?"

Riley felt the sting in her heart intensify. She took a moment to gather her thoughts, fighting the tears welling in her eyes. "It's not that simple. My connection to Caleb isn't just a distraction. It's... profound. I have to figure out what happened to him. I feel this driving need to help him."

Ethan leaned against a tree, his frustration replaced by bewildered hurt. "You think I can't understand what that feels like? I care about you, Riley. I want to be there for you."

"I care about you, too!" The confession slipped from her lips before she could restrain it. "But I can't just ignore what's happening. The ghost world—it's real, and I'm..."

For a moment, the air between them thickened with unspoken tension. Riley wasn't sure how to finish her thought. She wasn't just feeling the warmth of Ethan's presence; she also felt the fierce bond growing with Caleb.

"You're what?" Ethan pressed.

"Afraid," she finally admitted. "Afraid of missing out on something real with you because of..." She hesitated. "Because of this invisible weight, I feel. Caleb needs me."

A charged silence lingered. Ethan's shoulders relaxed slightly, his voice dropped to a hesitant whisper. "And what about what I need?"

The earnestness in his tone struck a chord deep within her. "You... you mean a lot to me, Ethan. I really like you." Her heart raced, spilling forth emotions tangled and raw. "But sometimes it feels like there's something connecting me to Caleb beyond myself. It's like a magnet drawing me to him. I can't just turn away from that."

Ethan's jaw tightened, his eyes searching hers. "So, what do I do? Watch you chase after shadows while I stand here hoping you notice me?"

Riley felt the suffocating reality of their situation crashing down around her. The night stretched like an endless expanse filled with uncertainty. "I never wanted you to feel like that, I don't—"

"Maybe you should just choose, then. If this ghost means that much to you, what's stopping you from... from going after him?"

The accusation cut deeper than she expected. Heat rose in her cheeks as vulnerability loomed large. "I want to understand Caleb, and I don't want to lose you."

An unexpected smile ghosted across Ethan's lips, almost reminiscent of the warmth from the fire. "You can't have both, Riley."

The finality of his words hung in the air, a truth she couldn't deny. She felt the heaviness of her heart settle into her stomach as the rift stretched wider between them. Their breaths echoed in the stillness, while the distant sounds of laughter that once surrounded them faded into a haunting silence. Subtle as a whisper, Caleb's essence lingered just beyond the lantern's glow.

Riley looked away, the ache in her chest throbbing like a wound laid bare. Ethan took a step closer, his expression softening. "I guess I'm just a little selfish—wanting your full attention. Is that too much to ask?"

And just like that, the air between them shifted again, but the connection she desperately sought felt frayed and fragile. As Riley gazed into Ethan's eyes, the warmth she craved mingled incongruously with the haunting presence lingering still so close.

"Ethan…" she whispered, uncertain how to bridge the gap that had formed, knowing this wasn't just a simple choice but rather a struggle that could only lead to turmoil.

8
the deepening bond

Riley lay on her bunk in the sparsely furnished cabin, the soft chorus of crickets and the occasional rustle of leaves outside providing a backdrop to her swirling thoughts. The light from the dying embers in the fireplace flickered in the corners of the room, and the air grew cooler, thick with a sense of anticipation.

She turned restlessly beneath her blankets, the events of the day replaying in her mind. Ethan's concerned words echoed, filling her with both warmth and confusion. His smile flashed across her thoughts, juxtaposed with Caleb's haunting presence that lingered in the edges of her memory. It felt like a tug-of-war inside her, where longing and fear collided head-on. Who was she now, teetering on the precipice of two worlds—one filled with laughter and connection, the other steeped in lost emotions and unresolved stories?

Just as the weight of her thoughts threatened to drown her, a sudden chill swept through the cabin, lingering at the nape of her neck. *That could only mean one thing…*

Riley sat up, instinctively scanning the darkened corners illuminated only by a sliver of moonlight. The night felt charged and still, as if the whole world paused to inhale. Her heart raced.

Then, in an instant, he appeared before her. Caleb materialized like a wisp of smoke, his translucent form glowing softly in the silver light. Riley's breath caught in her throat, a mix of awe and trepidation flooding her senses. She remembered his sorrowful eyes from their last encounter, the weight of his eternity binding him to this place. He hovered, ethereal and quiet, in the space between fantasy and reality, and her pulse quickened as she took in the sight of him.

"Caleb?" The name slipped from her lips, almost a question and a confirmation all at once.

With gentle precision, he stepped closer, an unspoken understanding passing between them like a bridge being forged in the dark. He tilted his head, an echo of a smile ghosting over his lips, but Riley could see the sorrow woven into his expression too. It was a delicate dance of light and shadow, and in that moment, she felt the weight of his longing seep into her bones.

"What do you want to tell me?" she whispered, her voice barely a tremor. She didn't need to speak loudly; the intimacy of the moment felt sacred as if the air itself could become a confidante.

Caleb extended a hand toward her, and it was instantly clear. He didn't mean to frighten her. His eyes held depth, mirroring the myriad emotions coursing through him. She found herself transfixed, aware that this moment was something profound. There was magic in the silence, a shared solitude that enveloped them like the cozy blankets around her shoulders. She desired to reach out, to bridge the gap between their worlds, but a pang of uncertainty gripped her.

His hand hovered just inches from her, ethereal light shimmering at its edges. It felt warm despite the chill that clung to the air, and Riley felt an overwhelming surge of empathy.

"What do you need?" The words slipped from her lips again, almost inaudible, breaking the silence as she dared to edge closer to him.

Caleb's shoulders slumped ever so slightly at her question, the longing twisting deeper in her chest. She wished she could pull him closer, anchor him like a lighthouse in the storm of his sorrow. His gaze fell to the floor, and an unspoken burden seemed to weigh upon him.

With an expression that hinted at struggles and memories long buried, he gestured towards the window. The moonlight illuminated dust motes dancing lazily in the dark, floating like lost thoughts in the stillness. Riley followed his gaze, and in that moment, she understood. He wished to share the world as he had once known it—alive with laughter, the warmth of human connection, and the vibrancy of summer nights filled with promise.

"Caleb..." she began, her breath hitching at the recognition of his pain. "You're not just a memory; you're someone who loved this place… who is still tied to it."

Suddenly, he stepped closer still, the space between them narrowing until the air crackled with energy. His expression shifted from sadness to a mix of hope and vulnerability, inviting her into the sanctum of his affections. The depth of his gaze sent shivers down her spine, igniting something deep within her—a connection that transcended the veil of life and death.

To be seen by him felt like being recognized in her entirety; every ghostly flicker of doubt she harbored was dispelled in his luminous presence. He lifted his hand and, with infinite care, brushed his fingers against her cheek. It felt like a sweet whisper, a promise of understanding that thrummed beneath her skin.

But with that touch came the looming shadow of Ethan. Riley's heart tangled in her chest—the raw energy of the moment reminded her of the magnetic pull she felt towards both Caleb and Ethan. Torn between two souls, she found herself teetering on the precipice of desire and regret.

"Caleb," she said softly, her voice trembling with sincerity, "I don't know how to help you… how to help us."

A flicker of sadness crossed his features, and for a brief second, it felt as if he were listening to the words beneath the surface—the fear that there might never be clarity, the struggle to find a way forward that wouldn't hurt anyone.

He inclined his head again, something poignant passing between them, deeper than any spoken words could express. She sensed the gravity of a story untold, one filled with dreams unfulfilled and emotions bottled up for too long. It was overwhelming, and Riley felt herself swimming in the depths of it all—Caleb's unyielding need for connection; her own blossoming feelings for Ethan, fragile yet real.

"Do you want me to help you find peace, Caleb?" she ventured, her voice barely above a whisper.

His gaze deepened—entreating, longing. It was a silent admission that the pull of his past was suffocating, but he also understood the implications of her question. If she stepped into the void with him, it meant unraveling the truths at Camp Willowood, and perhaps facing some uncomfortable realities lurking in the shadows of both their lives.

In all the twilight that bathed them, they exchanged a moment filled with heartache and understanding. Here in this cabin, their souls danced in the space between light and dark, yearning for something beyond words, yet tethered to their individual realities. The night spiraled around them, twinkling stars serving as witnesses to what could be, what might never be.

Caleb faded slowly, a whisper on the breeze, and Riley's heart clenched with the weight of their connection. As he vanished into the moonlight, the echoes of their unspoken bond hung heavy in the air, leaving her with lingering questions and an urgency she couldn't ignore. She sat in silence, the moon casting shadows that seemed to stretch endlessly beyond the cabin walls, wondering just how far she would go to keep his memory alive and to help him find the peace he had sought for so long.

* * *

RILEY TOSSED in turned in her bed, trying to get comfortable. The night was still and the crickets were loud. Riley felt that familiar whisp of wind again and naturally sat up to greet whoever was there. Caleb's ghostly form materialized before her, the moonlight catching his ethereal glow. On this occasion, he didn't seem playful; instead, a seriousness weighed heavily in his eyes.

He reached out, and Riley felt a wave of warmth wash over her. Instinctively, she grasped his outstretched hand. The cabin faded away, and suddenly they stood in a sunlit clearing. Laughter echoed around them, pleasantly jarring against the stillness of the night.

It was a scene from long ago—an idyllic summer day at Camp Willowood. Riley watched as Caleb, youthful and vibrant, played a game with a group of excited campers. His laughter was contagious, filling the air with pure joy as he rallied the campers to cheer for one another.

caleb - 1975

"Come on, you can do it!" Caleb encouraged a shy girl as she approached the climbing wall. The girl beamed, her nerves easing under his supportive gaze. He stood by, beaming with pride as she conquered the wall, raising her hands in triumph.

Riley felt a swell of warmth forming in her chest. "He was so happy," she murmured, captivated by the sight. This was a side of him she had yet to see, untouched by sorrow.

As the vision shifted, the campers, now adorned with colorful camp t-shirts, gathered around a campfire. Caleb leaned in with several other counselors, their voices blending with the crackling of the flames. They exchanged ghost stories, teasing each other, and to Riley's surprise, she found herself caught up in the warmth of their camaraderie.

"Did you hear the one about the old tree by the lake?" one counselor exclaimed. "They say it was home to a spirit who guarded the camp!"

Caleb chuckled, shaking his head, laughter dancing in his eyes. "That's just an old wives' tale." Yet, Riley could see the way his expression shifted slightly, a shadow crossing his features as if he felt a deeper connection to the story.

With each moment, Riley felt more entwined in the memories, as if she were another camper, sharing in the infectious joy and laughter. She witnessed Caleb as he motivated kids to sing while sitting on logs after sunset— his bright spirit lighting up the dimming day.

"Look! I'll start us off!" he would say, singing some goofy camp song, his voice strong and confident. The campers chimed in, their voices filling the night air.

Moments turned into minutes, and Riley felt tears prickling at the corners of her eyes. She understood now; this was what Caleb had missed for so long, a sense of belonging, of love and joy. Everything he couldn't grasp anymore, trapped in this otherworldly limbo.

As the last rays of sunlight faded, the vision softened, drawing them back out of that blissful memory. They returned to the cabin as the light dimmed and the warmth of joy was replaced with an echo of longing.

"CALEB..." Riley whispered, her heart heavy with empathy, overwhelmed by emotions. She quickly wiped away the tears that she couldn't fully comprehend, and looked at him—his translucent form flickering like the dying embers of a fire.

He turned his gaze towards her, an unspoken connection knitting them closer. Caleb's brow furrowed, and a sadness etched across his features. "What you saw...it was my life, my existence—full of laughter and love. I never wanted to be just a memory."

"I can't imagine what it must've been like," Riley replied, her voice barely above a whisper, aching for his pain. "To be thrust into this... eternity, without closure."

"Every moment since that day has haunted me," Caleb confessed, his voice resonating with a deep echo. "I see them all—my campers, my friends, but they can't see me. They're moving on with their lives, and I'm left with an unquenchable thirst for connection."

Riley's heart thumped painfully in her chest as she absorbed his words. She realized that the bond they shared went beyond their encounters; he had been reaching out to her not just as a ghost, but as someone who needed a friend, someone to remember him for who he truly was.

"I want to help you, Caleb." Her voice trembled with earnestness. "You deserve to be remembered, not forgotten. But how can I do that?"

"Help me find the truth." His eyes flashed with desperation. "There are things that need to be revealed, pieces of my story I want told. I never had a chance to say goodbye properly. No one knows what really happened. I just want... I just want to be free."

His words hung in the air, heavy with significance, as the weight of his emotions bore down on Riley. The intensity of his longing radiated through her, amplifying the sadness that had crept into her heart.

Every word he had spoken resonated within her, amplifying her own desire to understand—not just Caleb's history, but also, the world that lay between them. She looked into his sorrowful eyes, feeling a pull far beyond the gravity of mere curiosity; it was an urge to understand the depths of his pain and offer him solace.

"I'll help you," she promised, though uncertainty laced her resolve. "Together, we can find the truth."

Caleb regarded her with appreciation, his gaze softening slightly. "Thank you, Riley. Understanding will start to heal what's broken... for both of us."

Riley felt a swell of emotions stir within her. She inhaled slowly, taking in the weight of their promise and the weight of her own conflicting feelings. Simply finding truth for Caleb could lead her down a complicated path.

But as she looked at him—her ghostly companion, so captivating yet burdened by regret—the possibility settled into her heart like a soothing balm. In that moment, all that mattered was Caleb's silent plea for remembrance.

Without warning, a chill swept through the cabin, a sensation that was increasingly familiar. A reminder of Ethan lingered in the back of her mind, creating a tugging sensation in her chest, predominantly tied to their blossoming connection.

Yet, standing with Caleb, she felt a fierce determination blossom within her. She couldn't ignore her burgeoning attraction to Ethan—it was sincere and warm, but it was also contrasted by the vital bond she was forging with Caleb, who needed her in a way that transcended the physical.

How could she reconcile the two connections?

Before Riley could dwell too long on the thought, Caleb's lips parted, drawing her attention back to him. "You understand, don't you? If my story remains untold, if I'm forgotten, I'll remain lost, wandering between realms. That's a fate I can't accept."

The urgency in his voice enveloped Riley, and as their eyes locked, the world around them faded into a stillness that allowed only for that shared gaze. In that moment, everything else—the intrigue of the camp, the ghost stories, and even her feelings for Ethan—felt far away. Here was Caleb, the boy whose life had been robbed away; more than a ghost, he had become a friend.

Through him, Riley sensed a duty to shed light on a tragic story that needed to be aired. And as their connection deepened, so too did the understanding that they shared—each grasping at pieces of a life that yearned for closure.

"But..." she murmured, her heart heavy with conflicting emotions. "I need you to promise me something in return. You can't let the regret of the past anchor you. You have to find a way to let go when the time comes."

Caleb nodded, emotion gleaming in his sorrowful eyes. "For you, I'll try. But Riley..." he paused, searching her gaze. "Just know that my longing will always exist. You remind me of all that I've lost."

* * *

RILEY SETTLED at the edge of the lake, the cool grass tickling her bare feet as she gazed up at the scattering of stars. Night enveloped Camp Willowood in a shroud of mystery, the vast sky twinkling above like glitter spilled across dark velvet. The chirping of crickets harmonized with the gentle lapping of water against the shore, creating a peaceful backdrop that momentarily calmed her swirling thoughts.

This spot had become her refuge—a place where the weight of expectations and responsibilities melted away, if only for a moment. Here, she could breathe and let the crisp evening air fill her lungs. Yet the beauty of her surroundings failed to erase the complexity of her heart. She felt torn between the captivating warmth of Ethan's laughter and the haunting sorrow that lingered in Caleb's presence.

"Such a beautiful night, don't you think?" Caleb's voice drifted through the air, echoing softly with an ethereal quality that brought a shiver to her spine. She turned, startled but immediately comforted by his presence. His ghostly figure hovered just a few feet away, the soft glow of moonlight illuminating the contours of his translucent form.

"Yeah, it is," she replied, her voice barely above a whisper. The space between them felt charged, filled with the unspoken connection that had grown stronger since their first encounter. Riley's heart raced, drawn not only to the boy who stood before her but also to the weight of their shared circumstances. "You like to surprise me."

Caleb smiled, "I do?"

Riley shook her head and kicked up water with her feet. "Yes, you do."

Caleb stepped closer, a tentative smile breaking through his sorrowful demeanor. "I used to love nights like these. The stories, the laughter, the dreams." His eyes glimmered, reflecting the starlight, hinting at the vibrant memories that still pulsed beneath the surface of his existence. "They felt limitless."

Riley focused on his gaze, the depth of those haunted eyes pulling her into a world where time stood still. "What were your dreams?" she asked, unable to hide the curiosity threading through her voice.

He looked away momentarily as if searching the dark water for an answer. "I wanted to be someone who made a difference—my brother went to Vietnam, and I wanted to protest the war. I wanted to teach kids—inspire them to see the magic in the world. "

The weight of his words hung in the air, heavy and vivid. "You are remembered, Caleb. You have not been forgotten." The sincerity in her tone ignited something inside her—a flicker of determination. "I'll make sure people know your story."

He turned to her, an earnest glimmer in his eyes that sparked a warmth in her chest. "Do you really mean that? It's been so long since I've felt anyone care."

Riley nodded, heart pounding as she felt the enormity of their moment. She wanted to reach out, to bridge the gap between their worlds. Caleb's presence cloaked her in an aura of understanding, urging her to dive deeper into the mystery of his life. "I promise I'll find a way to help you," she whispered, her voice steady and resolute.

A gentle breeze swirled around them, lifting her hair and sending ripples across the lake's surface, reflecting the stars scattered overhead. At that moment, their unspoken bond began to weave an intricate tapestry between them—a connection that transcended the chasm of life and death.

Caleb took a step closer, his hand reaching out. An electric energy crackled in the air as her heart raced, drawn to him like a moth to a flame. His fingers hovered just above her own, the proximity creating a sensation of warmth, yet Riley sensed the earthiness of his sorrow grounding them both.

"I miss the simple things," he said, his voice low and tremulous. "The laughter of my friends. The moments spent around a campfire, the way the darkness felt like it could hold anything."

She ached to comfort him, to share in the moments he had lost—moments that now belonged to a past where he had once lived. "How did it all go wrong? You had so much to give."

Caleb glanced toward the water, the flickering light of the stars reflecting in his eyes. "Jealousy, rivalry... I had a friend, someone I looked up to. But competition can twist even the closest bonds into something dark. One moment changed everything."

Riley's heart sank at the weight of his pain. She could see it in his eyes, that momentary flicker of despair that threatened to pull him back into the shadows of his past. It ignited a fire inside her, one that wanted to fight for him, to understand the past that chained him to this place. "I want to help you find closure," she insisted, pouring her urgent sincerity into every word.

Caleb's expression softened, and it felt like the air shifted between them, growing denser, yet lighter somehow. "I'd like that," he murmured, a smile breaking through his sorrow. In that moment, Riley felt something shift within her, the connection binding them growing more profound.

As she reached out, their fingers almost touching, a surge of energy surged through her, radiating from the point of their contact—yet their hands never met. Time slowed and the world faded, leaving only the two of them suspended between the realms of existence. It felt as if the stars themselves held their breath, drawn into the electric moment.

"I'll find a way to make it right," she repeated, her heart echoing the promise she made to him. "I promise."

"Thank you," Caleb whispered, sadness and hope swirling behind his gaze as they shared a glance filled with unspoken understanding.

The calming sounds of the night surrounded them, yet the air crackled with the weight of their fragile connection. Even as Riley felt Caleb's intense longing for freedom and closure, her mind couldn't shake the awareness that each moment spent with him pulled her further from Ethan, whose warmth and laughter had brought her joy.

Yet, in that sacred space between life and death, she embraced the pull of her heart. The moon hung high and heavy above them, illuminating her resolve as though acknowledging the gravity of the promise she made.

As the stars twinkled like distant dreams scattered across infinity, Riley felt empowered. She was ready to embrace the supernatural journey ahead, acutely aware of the emotional complexity it carried.

a night to remember

Riley stood among her friends, swirling ribbons in vibrant hues around the trees that bordered the clearing. Camp Willowood exuded an energy that hummed in the air, palpable and electric. Laughter erupted from various corners as campers adorned the space with colorful banners, twinkling string lights, and handmade crafts that spoke of summer creativity. The sun dipped on the horizon, casting a warm glow over the festivities to come, and matching the excitement in every teenager's heart.

But for Riley, the thrill was clouded by turmoil. She yanked a handful of ribbons tighter, her thoughts tangling effortlessly like the string in her hand. Each laughter rang like a bell, pulling her attention to Ethan, who flitted between groups, his sandy brown hair catching the light. He moved with an easy confidence, engaging everyone with his charm.

Riley observed him from the edge of the chaos, watching as his blue eyes sparkled with mischief. A fleeting pang of envy stirred in her chest, clashing with the warmth of her fond memories with him. She should be happy, she reminded herself. Ethan was everything she had hoped for—a perfect summer distraction, someone who was full of life and laughter. But alongside that light, Caleb's shadow loomed, a soft melancholy that tugged at her mind and heart.

Some of her friends joined in a jovial dance, spinning happily, carefree with the moment. Riley knew she should join them, lose herself in the music, and indulge in this fleeting summer joy. Yet, she felt anchored, pulled back into her thoughts, as the chill of Caleb's presence lingered in the back of her mind like a whisper.

As she tied another ribbon to a tree branch, voices intermingled around her, and the sound of a distant guitar strumming added a lively soundtrack. The atmosphere beckoned for laughter and joy, but Riley stood still, her heart feeling like it was caught between two worlds. She caught fleeting glances of Caleb in her mind—his ghostly form surrounded by the flickering shadows of the camp, his sadness palpable even amidst the comfort of the camp's allure.

"Riley! Come join us!" one of her cabinmates called out, their voice buoyant. But Riley barely heard them, her focus shifting back to Ethan, who now entertained a gaggle of younger campers with a mock dance-off. He flashed that irresistible smile, igniting a flutter in her stomach that she found difficult to ignore. It was the kind of smile that made her wish they were dancing, lost in a simpler moment.

Still, Caleb's presence loomed with insistence, wrapping around her heart like mist. She clutched the ribbon in her hands, uncertainty swirling inside her. How could she embrace this celebration while a part of her was tethered to a ghost? How could she dance freely with one young man when another—a boy with no physical form—needed her?

"Hey, Riley!" The sound of Ethan's voice cut through her thoughts. He approached her through the thrumming excitement, his swagger effortless as he caught her eye. Something in his demeanor sparked warmth in her chest. In that moment, it felt like the chaos slowed, and they were the only two people in the world.

"Can I commandeer your help for a second?" he asked, his tone playful.

"Sure," she replied, trying to shake off the weight of her inner turmoil.

"Let's get this tent over there a little more festive." With a grin, he gestured to a small pavilion that appeared sparse and underwhelming compared to the vibrancy surrounding them.

As they approached the tent, Riley couldn't help but notice how his energy pulled her in, drawing her closer to him without effort. They draped colorful lights around the structure, Ethan's hands moving deftly as he chatted about the games planned for the evening. They worked seamlessly, laughter flowing between them, emboldening Riley's spirit.

"So… save a dance for me tonight?" Ethan asked suddenly, glancing at her with earnest eyes.

A rush of excitement flared within Riley as the words settled in her chest. She felt the flutter of her heartbeat, her cheeks warming at the prospect. She nodded, her excitement almost palpable. "Definitely! I wouldn't miss it."

His smile widened, and her heart soared. But an undertow of uncertainty washed over her. As much as she craved this connection, memories of Caleb tugged at her conscience. Would she be dancing only with Ethan, or would Caleb's ghost linger at the edges of their joy? She hated the idea of splitting herself between the two.

"Awesome," Ethan beamed, brushing a lock of hair away from his forehead. "Let's make this a night to remember. I've got a feeling it'll be legendary." He turned back to the pavilion, his carefree attitude grounding her.

Riley busied herself tying the last few ribbons, but her thoughts drifted. Frosty whispers from Caleb brushed against her mind. What did he think of her newfound bond with Ethan? Did he feel betrayed by her laughter and the warmth of living flesh when he had never known warmth since his tragic night?

The chill against her skin was a reminder of the other side— of longing and lost connections.

A playful shove jolted her from her thoughts as one of her friends stumbled into her, causing her to drop an armful of decorations. "Oops! Sorry!" they laughed, but Riley barely registered it as her mind continued to spiral.

As the sun began to set, casting a kaleidoscope of colors across the sky, the camp erupted in a chorus of celebration. Campers gathered together, exchanging stories, showcasing dance moves, and embracing the joy of the night's festivities.

Feeling a weight in her chest, Riley stashed the ribbons in her bag, staring at the vibrant commotion. Ethan was already swept up in the excitement, and all she could do was stand on the periphery, the two different corners of her heart pulling her in opposite directions.

With every laugh that echoed through the air, she felt more divided.

"Hey!" Ethan's voice broke through. He waved her over, excitement lighting his features. She felt the pull of him as he stood among campers, gesturing her to join. But just as she took a step forward, a shiver coursed through her. It was a chill she had learned to associate with Caleb's presence.

Riley's heartbeat quickened as she caught sight of shadows dancing at the edge of her vision. A spectral glow flickered amid the trees, and something like sorrow mixed with yearning tightened in her chest. She paused, glancing back in a moment of hesitation, feeling the conflict within her clawing for attention.

Ethan's voice called again, brimming with life. "Come on, Riley, let's take this night head-on!"

That laughter and light beckoned her forward, but Caleb's ghostly figure lingered just out of reach, still and silent. She felt trapped between two worlds, each pulling her heart apart. This party, with its laughter and rhythm, was alive in a way that tethered her to Ethan. Yet the lingering sorrow of Caleb haunted her, a reminder of the fragility of connections lost and yet found again.

"Riley?" Ethan's tone shifted, concern threading through his excitement. His smile faltered as he stepped closer, studying her face.

The air hummed thick with anticipation and emotion, but tonight was meant for celebration. She could feel it in her bones, the music, the energy, and the undeniable electricity in the air. She inhaled deeply, taking in the scents of pine, warmth, and the camaraderie shared among campers.

"Okay," she whispered to herself, resolving to embrace the beauty of the present, even as her heart clung to the past.

For a flickering moment, Riley glanced towards the shadows that hinted at a lingering presence, feeling the ghost of Caleb push at the edges of her thoughts. But with that, she took a step toward Ethan, embracing the excitement of the moment, determined to participate in this whirlwind of life and laughter—if only for a night.

AS NIGHT FELL over Camp Willowood, the world transformed. The sky deepened into shades of indigo, dotted with shimmering stars. From the heart of the camp, the glow of a bonfire flickered, casting warmth across the gathered campers. Laughter and chatter wove a tapestry of sounds, the joyous spirit radiating through the air. The scent of pine mingled with the faint aroma of toasted marshmallows, enveloping Riley in a sensation of carefree magic.

Riley stood with her friends, feeling the pulsing energy around her. They swayed to the music drifting from the camp speakers, a lively mix that made everyone want to move. So much excitement filled the night, and in that moment, Riley momentarily forgot the weight of her thoughts—Caleb and the mystery of his past fading into the background.

"Come on, Riles! Come dance with us!" one of her cabinmates called, pulling Riley into the throng of vibrant energy. They twirled together as giggles erupted, the carefree atmosphere sweeping Riley up in its infectious grip. She relished the moment, spinning and laughing, letting the excitement wash over her like the warm breeze that rustled the trees overhead.

As the festivities reached their peak, Ethan stepped into her line of sight. He stood at the fringe of the crowd, his sandy hair tousled and that signature smile lighting up his face. He caught Riley's eye, extending his hand toward her with an inviting grin that stirred butterflies in her stomach.

"Want to dance?" His warm voice cut through the cacophony, making Riley's heart race. She nodded, unable to suppress the smile that spread across her face.

As they made their way to the center of the makeshift dance floor, the music shifted to a slower tempo, the atmosphere taking on a more intimate feel. The campers around them paired up, creating a whirl of movement beneath the starlit sky. Ethan took her hand, gently guiding her into an embrace, pulling her close as they began to sway.

Riley could feel the heat radiating off him, and the world around them faded into a blur. Every sway of their bodies felt electric as if the universe had conspired to craft this moment for them. She met his gaze, and in those deep blue depths, she felt seen. Felt known. For just a moment, the connection between them seemed to magnify—a pulse that resonated between their hearts.

"Is this the part where you impress me with your dance moves?" Ethan teased, his voice smooth as honey, pulling her from her reverie.

Riley laughed, feeling both playful and shy. "I can definitely try," she said, pretending to rock side-to-side before shifting into a rhythm more of her own. The way Ethan watched her, admiration shining in his eyes, added a flutter to her step. She twirled, and he caught her, their bodies inches apart, laughter weaving through the air between them.

The way he leaned in closer, their faces inches apart, made Riley's heart race. The music faded, and all she could focus on was the warmth of his breath against her skin, intoxicating her senses. Riley could feel the pull of gravity between them, the world narrowing until it was just them beneath the vast expanse of glittering stars.

Ethan leaned in, and in the next breath, their lips met—soft, tentative at first, igniting into something more. The kiss sent a thrill down Riley's spine, raising goosebumps on her arms despite the warmth surrounding her. Time seemed to stand still. The world around them disappeared completely, and the fire crackled gently in the background, adding a soft glow to the moment.

But as quickly as it began, it ended. They pulled away, breathless and slightly dazed. Riley's cheeks flushed; she looked up at Ethan, searching for signs of doubt in his eyes, but all she found was joy.

"Wow," he whispered, a genuine smile lighting up his face. "That was… unexpected."

"Definitely unexpected," Riley agreed, her heart pounding wildly in her chest. Excitement mixed with emotion, warming her from the inside out. Just then, however, a subtle shift in the atmosphere pricked at her instinct.

Riley's eyes flickered to the edge of the firelight. The moment felt euphoric, yet haunting in another way. There, cloaked in shadow, she spotted Caleb. His translucent form seemed to shimmer with melancholy beneath the glowing stars, eyes wide and filled with unspoken feelings—longing, sorrow, desperation. A knot tightened in her chest, and she felt a pang of guilt wash over her.

The joyous sensations from the dance faded, overshadowed by the heartache she hadn't fully faced. Caleb stood so close —yet so far, encapsulated in an ethereal separation Riley couldn't breach. It tugged at her, a reminder of the promise she had made to help him find closure.

Ethan followed her gaze, brow furrowing as he sensed a change in her demeanor. "Riley? What's wrong?" His voice cut through the cloud of discord, grounding her in the present.

"Nothing," she blurted, but the denial felt flimsy against the weight of her emotions. She couldn't shake the image of Caleb—his sad smile and the depth of his sorrow.

"Are you sure? You look a little…" Ethan hesitated, searching for the right word. "Distant."

Caleb's form shifted, fading into the shadows, yet Riley felt his presence lingering against her skin. She clenched her fists, torn between the overwhelming affection for Ethan and the echo of Caleb's silent plea.

"I'm okay. Just a lot on my mind," she finally replied, a soft smile returning to her face. Ethan's concern tugged at her heart, and she couldn't bear to cloud the magic of the moment, even if it felt like a delicate thread binding her to two separate worlds.

"Okay," Ethan said slowly, but his eyes remained worried. He brought her hand up to his lips, pressing a soft kiss against her knuckles, a sweet gesture that sent warmth flowing through her veins. "Just know I'm here if you want to talk."

"Thanks, Ethan," she murmured, grateful for his patience, but her heart skittered. Still, she couldn't deny what loomed just beyond their shared happiness.

As they walked back into the soft glow near the bonfire, Riley felt Caleb's absence keenly, a haunting reminder that the complexities of her heart were far from over. She couldn't ignore either of them, couldn't separate the pieces of her connection to Caleb from the blossoming relationship with Ethan.

* * *

THE BONFIRE CRACKLED CHEERFULLY as campers danced under the canopy of stars, casting flickering shadows across the lively gathering. Laughter mingled with music, the air alive with the sweet smell of roasted marshmallows and pine. Riley felt the warmth of the evening envelop her, but an unsettling mixture of exhilaration and tension churned within her.

Ethan stepped forward, his sandy hair catching the light in a way that made him appear almost ethereal. His smile, bright and inviting, drew her in, and for a moment, the world faded around them. "Tonight's been amazing," he said, the sincerity in his tone making her heart flutter. "I've never seen the camp come alive like this."

"Yeah, it really has," she replied, her voice almost lost in the bustling echoes of the party. Her cheeks flushed, not just from the warmth of the fire but from being so close to him. Every flicker in his deep blue eyes seemed to pull her in, igniting an undeniable chemistry between them.

As if sensing the charged atmosphere, Ethan took a step closer, the space between them dissolving. "Would you mind getting away from the crowd for a sec? I want to talk to you—just us."

"What do you mean?" Riley's heart raced, a mix of excitement and apprehension swirling inside her. She couldn't shake the feeling that this was a pivotal moment, yet her thoughts still raced back to Caleb's sorrowful presence watching from the shadows of her mind.

Ethan gently tugged on her hand, leading her away from the jubilant celebration and toward the edge of the lake. The sound of laughter faded, replaced by the soft lapping of water against the shore and the rustling of trees swaying in barely-there summer breezes. It was tranquil, momentarily masking the chaos of emotions inside her.

Once they reached a secluded spot, Ethan released her hand, though his warmth lingered like an echo. He turned toward her, his expression soft, thoughtful. "I just wanted to say… I really like you, Riley. You've been a breath of fresh air at Camp Willowood. I guess…I feel like tonight has opened a door for us. Maybe we could explore what's between us?"

In that moment, the world around them dimmed, crystallizing the whirlwind of emotions they both shared. The lake shimmered under the stars, the silhouettes of the trees framing this intimate scene. But just when Riley felt herself leaning into the warmth of Ethan's offer, Caleb's voice pierced through the fog of her heart's contentment, echoing in her mind with familiar urgency.

She recalled how his ghostly presence had implored her for understanding, for closure. The two worlds felt more distant than ever—Ethan's living warmth calling her towards a future, while Caleb's pain reminded her of an unfinished story clamoring for resolution.

"Ethan, I…" Riley hesitated, the weight of her connection to both boys pulling her in diametrically opposing directions. "I think you're really special too, but I—"

"Riley…" He stepped closer, searching her eyes, his voice barely above a whisper. "What's going on?"

Tension coiled tighter in her chest. Was she willing to step away from Caleb's unfinished business for this living spark? The joy in Ethan's gaze challenged the shadows that had settled around her heart. Torn between two lives, she felt paralyzed, the enormity of her choice closing in around her.

With the first explosive crack of fireworks lighting up the sky, she felt the moment snap at her heartstrings. The vibrant colors blossomed overhead—streaks of red, green, and gold—casting vibrant patterns that reflected in her wide eyes.

"Can we pause here? Just for a minute?" she said suddenly, her breath escaping in a rush as she stepped back from him, desperate for space. She needed to gather her thoughts before she could answer him—and address the truth buried deep inside.

"Why?" Ethan asked, frustrated.

"Why?" she whispered to the water as if it might hold the answers—answers swirling just beneath the surface. "Why can't I just choose?"

The stars blinked down thoughtfully, and for an eerie moment, she felt as if Caleb might materialize behind her in answer. She steadied her breath, trying to quiet the rising storm in her chest. All those moments they shared—their unspoken connection, the weight of his longing eyes now etched there in her mind. If she turned away, would she be abandoning him?

Just as her heart began to settle, Riley turned slightly, ensuring Ethan wouldn't overhear her thoughts, addressing the emptiness that loomed in her heart in a quiet murmur, "Caleb, I promised I would help you. I can't forget that. You deserve to be remembered."

The stillness of the night wrapped around her as if to embrace her decision. Just then, above the sound of crackling fireworks lighting up the sky, a breeze breezed past, bringing an ethereal whiff of something familiar. Riley closed her eyes, picturing Caleb's ghostly gaze, the yearning emanating from him in waves.

With her heart pounding in her chest, she straightened and turned back toward Ethan, who waited patiently, brows furrowed, as if trying to decipher the conflict on her face.

"Riley?" His voice was softer now, a mix of concern and curiosity as he closed the distance between them again.

Just as she opened her mouth to speak, a firework exploded, scattering bright sparks around them. In that dazzling moment, the weight of her decision loomed large, brimming with potential and heartache. Choices awaited, desperately woven into the fabric of this summer beneath the stars.

One choice would lead her down the path toward new love, while the other would connect her to a ghost longing for peace.

10
unraveling the mystery

The sun streamed through the dusty windows of the camp library, casting a warm glow on the scattered papers and books. Riley leaned over the large wooden table, her fingers brushing against the faded spine of an old yearbook. Determination flickered in her blue eyes; she felt it in her bones that the truth about Caleb's past lay within these walls.

"Okay, everyone, we need to focus," Riley instructed, straightening her back as she gathered her friends around her. "There has to be more than what we've found so far."

Sam, one of her cabinmates, flipped through a stack of yellowed newspapers. "I mean, it's just a ghost story, right? You really think we'll find anything that matters?"

"A ghost story that might involve a tragedy!" Riley shot back, her voice firmer than intended. "Caleb deserves to be remembered. This isn't just some fun summer project for me."

Her friends shared glances, uncertainty creeping into their expressions.

"Riley's right," called out Ethan, a reassuring tone in his voice as he stepped in close. "Let's find out the truth. It could help us understand why Caleb... why he's still here. You know, maybe it's something serious."

Motivated by Ethan's encouragement, Riley's resolve strengthened. She flipped through the yearbook, pausing on an image of a much younger Caleb, with a wide grin and a hint of mischief dancing in his eyes. It felt surreal, staring at a photograph of someone who had become such an integral part of her summer experience, even if he was extremely ethereal.

As they continued to sift through the archives of old newspapers and journals, Riley discovered a series of articles detailing the camp's old traditions. She pushed aside dusty volumes that whirled to life under their enthusiasm. Old memories captured in paper rustled as they uncovered stories of friendships and summer romances among the counselors. Yet, something gnawed at Riley— she needed to know more, and she couldn't shake the feeling that something monumental slipped through the crevices of time.

"Hey, check this out," whispered Liz, the quietest of their group, who usually kept to herself behind her curtain of dark hair. She handed Riley a thin envelope, its edges frayed with age.

Riley carefully opened it. Inside, she discovered a neatly folded, faded letter, the ink slightly smudged from the years.

"What does it say?" Sam asked incredulously, his voice cutting through the whispers of the library.

Taking a deep breath, Riley unfolded the letter, excitement mixed with apprehension bubbling in her chest. She started reading aloud.

"Dear Mom and Dad..."

The words painted a picture of Caleb's hopes for the summer, revealing dreams of laughter, the joy of working with campers, and plans to help with the annual canoe trip.

"I can't wait to show the younger kids how to swim! It's such a great feeling to inspire them,"

she read, her voice losing inflection as the enchantment of the moment gripped her.

> *"This summer is going to be incredible... I have dreams of becoming a teacher. I want to make a difference and ensure our campers have memories they'll cherish."*

Riley's heart thudded harder as she continued to read, feeling the vibrance of life coursing through each word. The excitement spilling from the pages felt tangible, filling the library with warmth. But then a shadow passed through the room, darkness creeping in.

Halfway through the letter, the tone shifted. Caleb's words began to reflect doubt.

> *"I feel like I have so much to prove... I've got big shoes to fill after what happened last year. I hope everyone here can see me for who I want to be—not who I once was."*

Riley stopped, glancing up from the letter. Around the table, her friends wore expressions of shock and sorrow, the fleeting joy of a bright future now marred by an invisible tragedy.

"That's... so sad," Liz murmured, her voice almost a whisper.

"Yeah, but it's just— wait. What do you mean 'what

happened last year'?" Sam interjected, a frown pinching his features.

Riley's heart raced as she looked at the letter again, realizing they had jogged hard against the walls of an unresolved narrative. "That's what we need to find out," she replied, her voice strained.

"But why? It's just a ghost story! You can't honestly think you're gonna prove anything?" Sam crossed his arms, skepticism etched on his face.

Riley narrowed her eyes, feeling heat bloom in her cheeks. "He's not just a ghost. He... he had a life. Dreams. A family. You can't just dismiss that."

"The rest of us have families too, you know," Sam shot back. "What's next? Are we going to start holding seances? This is getting ridiculous!"

"Just because you don't care doesn't mean the rest of us don't!" Riley snapped, frustration bubbling to the surface.

"Riley, calm down," Liz interjected softly. "I get what you're trying to do, but—"

"No! You don't get it!" Riley's heart raced as doubt flooded in. "He's been communicating with me! I have witnessed the truth of his existence! We need to honor him."

Ethan stepped forward, a calming presence amid the rising tension. "Guys, what if we just set aside the skepticism for a second? Whether or not we believe in ghosts, Caleb *was* real. His life mattered. Maybe his story is tied to why he has remained here. It's worth exploring."

"You really think we're going to solve a mystery from decades ago, just because of some letter?" Sam grumbled.

"Isn't that enough?" Riley challenged. "There is power in a person's story. If we don't chase the truth, we will let him slip through the cracks forever."

The air grew heavy with silence. The intensity of the group's conflicting emotions hung palpably, intertwining uncertainty with determination.

"Alright," Liz finally said, her voice timid yet firm. "Let's figure out what happened to Caleb. But… we have to do this together."

Their eyes shifted from Sam to Riley, and the momentary fissure began to close.

Riley nodded, determined. "Let's find the truth about what really happened."

* * *

RILEY SAT cross-legged on the cool wooden floor of the old cabin. The rhythmic creaking of the aged structure had morphed into a soothing backdrop, blending seamlessly with the gentle rustle of trees outside. She placed a solitary candle in front of her, lighting it with hands that trembled slightly from both anticipation and an undercurrent of anxiety. The soft flicker cast dancing shadows around the room, transforming the familiar space into something more mystical, more alive.

She closed her eyes, taking a deep breath. The scent of cedar and melting wax filled her lungs, grounding her in the moment as she cleared her mind of the cacophony of worries—a burgeoning romance with Ethan, the fervor of uncovering Caleb's tragic story, and the push-and-pull of her emotions. Everything fell away until only the cool night air kissed her skin, and the heartbeat of the camp pulsed faintly beyond the walls.

No distractions, no noise. Just her and the beyond.

"Caleb," she whispered into the stillness, letting the name linger in the air as she visualized him, desperate for connection, for the truth. "I'm here."

The room remained silent, save for the soft crackle of the candle wick. Riley focused harder, allowing the warmth of the flame to envelop her. She summoned her mediumship abilities, tapping into the energy that spanned between realms, essentially inviting Caleb's spirit into her circle.

And then it happened.

A sudden rush of cold air wrapped around her, distinct and clear. In that moment, Riley felt less alone. A flicker at the edge of her vision caught her attention. As she opened her eyes, Caleb materialized before her, more vivid than she had ever seen him. His translucent form glowed ethereally in the candlelight, each flicker emanating from within like a beacon of sorrow and yearning.

"Caleb," Riley breathed, her heart quickening. "I want to understand."

His gaze pierced her with an intensity that made her shiver, bouncing between sadness and a desperate hope for understanding. No longer playful, Caleb's presence bore the weight of his past. He reached out, his hand hovering above hers, a gesture that spoke volumes, igniting a yearning in Riley to bridge their worlds.

Suddenly, the atmosphere shifted. The candlelight flickered violently, and everything around her faded to black before returning with blinding clarity. They were no longer in the cabin; they stood amidst the haunting beauty of the camp decades ago—a glimpse into a past now shrouded in mist.

Riley looked around, her breath catching. She recognized the dilapidated cabin where Caleb had once worked, vibrant and full of laughter. Voices echoed like music, muffled yet melodious, inviting her to get closer.

"See it," Caleb whispered, his voice an echo that reached through time. "Feel it."

Suddenly, a series of vivid memories unfolded before her. Campers frolicked around, laughter filling the air. Caleb moved between groups, youthful and full of hope, tossing a frisbee and joking with others. A kind smile graced his face, and for an instant, Riley felt the raw joy in the air—unrestrained, contagious.

But shadows loomed on the periphery. With each passing vision, the mood shifted as glimpses of tension crept into the memories. Rivalry sparked like a flame; discontent brewed among campers and counselors, whispering jealousy and misunderstandings that pulsed in the air like a storm. Riley saw Caleb with a fellow counselor, whose face twisted into an ugly scowl when their interactions became too friendly.

Scenes flickered rapidly, each telling a part of the story, each one revealing a layer of Caleb's anguish—an unrelenting sense of entrapment. He was adored by his campers, yet the jealousy of someone he trusted clamped down on him like a vise.

"Why?" Riley cried out, desperation seeping into her words. "Why did it have to end like this?"

Tears filled her eyes as Caleb faced her, his grief welling with a deep sadness that hung in the air between them. He pointed to the unfolding scene—snippets of arguments, threats hidden in careless whispers. She watched as he faced the very counselor who had felt bitterness towards him, their faces twisting with rage.

"Trapped in a cycle," Caleb murmured. "And those who loved me… they couldn't see. They couldn't know."

The unrelenting ache of his memories clawed at Riley's heart. "You didn't deserve this," she whispered, feeling the weight of the unresolved tragedy.

As if sensing her empathy, Caleb stepped closer, his essence radiating a somber warmth. The flickering candlelight surrounded them, merging their souls—a brief, tangible connection that transcended time.

"Face the truth, Riley," he urged, his voice haunted yet commanding. "Not just for me—but for you, for Ethan. You carry my story now."

Her mind raced, tangled with emotions. A potent mix of determination and empathy grew inside her. She understood now that this was bigger than her initial curiosity about a ghost; it was about injustice, closure, and healing. Caleb's pain pierced through her own heart, igniting a fire in her spirit—a pledge to seek justice in his memory.

Perhaps it wasn't only Caleb who needed resolution; maybe she would find clarity for herself too. The journey ahead wouldn't be straightforward, but it was her path to take.

"I promise, Caleb," she breathed in earnest. "I'll do everything I can to uncover the truth. You won't be forgotten."

He looked at her with sad regret, moving closer, the space between them charged with unspoken words. Their worlds felt intertwined, quiet yet energized by possibility. For the first time, Riley felt the profound importance of their connection—the realization that she would honor Caleb's life through her quest.

And just before she could fully grasp the weight of what this meant, the candle flickered again. The vision receded, giving way to the blackness of the cabin. Caleb's form shimmered, slowly fading as if the light of the moment was being snuffed out.

Riley's heart raced, and she lunged forward, desperate to hold on. "Caleb, please! Don't go! Please, tell me more!"

But only silence answered her.

RILEY GATHERED her friends in the library's hushed corners again, sunlight streaming through dusty windows, illuminating the musty smell of old paper and forgotten stories. The atmosphere grew serious as she set the scene for what she had to share. With her hands trembling slightly, she placed the faded letter on the table, the edges yellowed and frayed, a tangible piece of Caleb's past.

"Listen, I know this sounds crazy," she began, looking around at the skeptical faces surrounding her. "But this letter… it holds the dreams he had for that summer, plans that were cut short. He wanted to be someone, make a difference here."

Her friends leaned in, their curiosity piqued. Riley could see some of them soften, the light of intrigue flickering to life in their eyes.

Mia, who'd been the most dismissive of their ghostly pursuits, crossed her arms defensively, eyebrows raised. "And how exactly does a letter from a ghost help us? It's just words on a page. I mean, anyone can write a letter."

With a sigh, Riley pressed her palms against the table, steady. "That's the thing, Mia. It's not just a letter. It represents what he lost—a life, friends, things we take for granted. We need to uncover what really happened to him… not just to honor Caleb, but to find closure."

"Closure? For a ghost?" another friend, Jake, scoffed. "What's the point if he's… you know, dead? It's all just stories, Riley."

"Stop," Ethan interjected, his voice cutting through the rising tension. He stepped closer to the table, fiery determination in his gaze directed at his friends. "Riley is onto something. I've seen what's happening with her and Caleb. There's something real there. He deserves to be remembered."

Riley's heart raced, warmed by Ethan's support. She could feel a swell of camaraderie, her belief reaffirmed. "Exactly, Ethan. What if Caleb didn't just disappear? What if there was something deeper to his story? Rivalries, jealousies—the stuff that ruins lives. Just because we can't see it doesn't mean it didn't happen."

"So, what's the plan?" Mia asked, her tone shifting from skepticism to interest. "We can't just wander around like headless chickens asking random people about a ghost's backstory."

"Old counselors or locals," Riley proposed enthusiastically, her ideas flowing. "There might be historians or staff who were here when it happened. They could shed light on the kind of rivalries Caleb had, the relationships in the camp back then. We don't need direct evidence of Caleb himself, just the environment he was entangled in."

"Well, if we're doing this," Jake relented, running a hand through his hair, "let's do it properly. We need a timeline, a real plan. We can split up tasks. I can call my uncle—he writes for the local newspaper. He might know something about old camp stories."

"I'll scour more newspaper archives," Mia chimed in reluctantly, a hint of excitement breaking through her skepticism. "Who knows what we might find."

Riley locked eyes with Ethan, whose steadfast gaze spoke volumes. "And I'll try to reach out to the camp's oldest counselors still alive. They might have information on Caleb that could connect dots for us," he said.

The air crackled with newfound energy as they brainstormed together, scribbling notes and sharing ideas. Riley felt a shift in the atmosphere as her friends rallied around her, skepticism evaporating in the face of a shared purpose.

"I'll take charge of our interview questions. We need to go in there with clear intentions," Riley said, her voice steady. "Every detail might matter. If we can find something connecting Caleb to his peers, maybe we can discover who he meant when he wrote about jealousy."

As the group threw around ideas, the plan crystallized. They would research together, exploring the camp's history and Caleb's life, piecing together fragments of a narrative that lay buried beneath layers of time.

11
the struggle between worlds

Riley stood at the entrance of the small diner just outside of Camp Willowood, her heart racing as she glanced back at her friends. They were a mixed bag of emotions—anticipation hung in the air. The bell above the door jingled when they stepped inside, announcing their arrival in a place that felt steeped in time. The walls were lined with local memorabilia, photographs of campers long gone, and faded camp posters from decades past.

"Riley, are you sure about this?" Emily cast a wary glance around the diner, uneasy beneath the weight of the old stories that seemed to permeate the walls.

"We need to hear what Mrs. Mitchell has to say," Riley replied, crossing her arms. She understood Emily's skepticism, but this was a part of understanding Caleb's past. The mystery around his disappearance was too important to let fear hold them back.

Diane Mitchell, the former camp staff member, sat in a booth near the window, her sharp blue eyes watching them as they approached. She had a worn-out but composed air, each wrinkle on her face telling a story of countless summers spent nurturing campers into young adults. Being the camp's director for over two decades, Diane held a wealth of memories, some likely too painful to recall.

"Hello, Diane," Riley greeted, her voice steady but her insides tumbling with nerves. She slid into the booth opposite the woman, her friends following her lead.

"Hello, Riley, it's nice to meet you," Diane said, her tone holding a hint of nostalgia that softened the edges of her authoritative demeanor. "What brings you here?"

Riley took a deep breath. "We've been digging into the history of Camp Willowood, specifically about Caleb Whitaker. We were hoping you could help us understand what really happened to him."

Diane's expression shifted, shadowed with a hint of sorrow as she leaned back in her seat. "Caleb… such a bright young man." She briefly looked out the window, her gaze drifting as if searching for something lost. "What do you want to know?"

Riley exchanged nervous glances with her friends before looking back at Diane, determination flooding her veins. "Anything. We want to understand the circumstances surrounding his disappearance. People keep mentioning a rivalry between him and another counselor."

At the mention of rivalry, Diane seemed to bristle, her lips pressing into a tight line. "Rivalries often fester in competitive environments, especially among counselors eager to prove themselves. Caleb had a close friend, but he also had an escalating tension with a fellow counselor—Jake, if I remember correctly. It culminated in a competition both of them felt they had to win."

"Competition for what?" Emily asked, curiosity cracking her skepticism.

"For the favorite counselor role among those campers," Diane replied, her voice softening slightly. "It sounds trivial, but when you're a teenager—especially back in the 70s—it means *everything*. It was a summer filled with bullheaded pride and a desperate craving for approval."

"A competition gone wrong?" Riley's brow furrowed, the pieces of the puzzle shifting in her mind.

Diane grimaced. "Yes. On the night Caleb disappeared, there was a campfire event. The kind where everything is meant to inspire courage and camaraderie. But tensions ran high. The last few times Caleb and Jake faced off, their competition had turned sour. We'd had complaints from campers about the rivalry getting out of hand; angry words were exchanged, and Caleb mentioned feeling cornered. It wasn't just competition. There was a friendship betrayed, and things turned darker."

Riley could feel the chill of memories encasing the air around them, memories of youthful ambition twisting into something more ominous. "What do you mean by 'darker'?"

Diane leaned forward, lowering her voice. "I believe Caleb might have been set up. Or, at the least, manipulated into a confrontation that left him vulnerable. Jake had a temper, and he was jealous of Caleb's ability to connect with the campers."

The diner seemed to grow still as Diane continued, "There was passive aggression building up that summer. I remember overhearing snippets of conversations—whispered insults. That fateful night, I was overseeing the event and noticed Caleb was more on edge than usual. Just before he disappeared, I saw a shadowy figure off in the woods." Diane glanced at Riley, searching for understanding in the girl's eyes. "It was a feeling I couldn't shake. Something felt off."

Riley's heart raced. "You think it was Jake? That he… caused Caleb's disappearance?"

Diane shook her head, frustration flickering briefly across her features. "The camp had a rule against serious fights, and each counselor knew the stakes, but… the adrenaline sometimes took over. And it gets lost in the shuffle of young emotions. I can't know for sure, but given Caleb's state of mind, I wouldn't put it past Jake to escalate things."

Emily's face paled, and Riley looked at her friend, noticing the tension in her shoulders. For someone who had been skeptical all along, these revelations had shaken her resolve. "This is… a lot," Emily whispered, her voice trembling.

Diane regarded Emily, her expression softening. "We looked for months after his disappearance. Local law enforcement, countless search parties, even the FBI—but we could never find him."

Riley felt a swelling sense of empathy, resonating with the burden of Caleb's untold story. "We need to keep digging. Hear more about Jake, gather more evidence, whatever it takes. We owe it to Caleb."

As Diane nodded, a flicker of recognition passed between them, an unspoken commitment to uncovering buried truths. Riley glanced around the diner, her friends now captivated and engaged. They were all in this together, awakening to the reality of a life interconnected with loss and longing.

In that moment, something shifted within Riley; she felt validated, empowered by the resolve of her friends and the weight of Caleb's story that pressed against her heart. The pieces of Caleb's past were not just fragments; they were reminders of his vibrant life, lost but not forgotten. Everything about the investigation bore deeper meaning now—it was about unearthing buried emotions, lost connections, and reclaiming a narrative long silenced by tragedy.

"Let's regroup later and discuss a strategy, especially about Jake," Riley said, her tone firm. "This time, it'll be different. We won't let the past just fade away anymore."

* * *

RILEY STEPPED AWAY from the car, her heart pounding as she made her way back to camp. The crisp autumn air was a stark contrast to the emotional turmoil swirling within her. She glanced back at the vehicle, its driver nodding in acknowledgment, before moving toward the familiar path that led to the lake. Every step felt weighted, the tension in the air palpable as thoughts of Ethan and Caleb fought for her attention.

The water sparkled under the dappled sunlight, mirroring the chaotic mix of feelings roiling inside her. She felt drawn to the shoreline, where the ripples danced playfully, but her heart felt heavy with uncertainty. Today had revealed so many truths about the past, and yet it only deepened the divide between her and the two souls who held her heart captive.

As she stood at the water's edge, her mind played back the elderly staff member's words, each revelation echoing with the weight of Caleb's tragic story. This place was haunted, and more than ghosts wandered the paths that whispered of love, loss, and unresolved anguish. She took a deep breath, filling her lungs with the earthy aroma of the lake—a soothing reminder of her connection to nature and the life surrounding her. Yet it felt as if something else was nearby, a presence that clung to the air like a static charge.

And then he was there.

Caleb's figure emerged from the shadows, ethereal and luminous. His eyes, usually filled with warmth, now revealed an urgency that made Riley's heart race. He stepped closer, his translucent form shimmering in the afternoon light, and an invisible thread stretched between them, tugging at her heart.

"Riley," he whispered, his voice echoing with a haunting timbre. "You need to listen."

Her pulse quickened. She was torn between the desire to run into his comforting embrace and the instinct to retreat, to deny the inexplicable bond that tethered her to this ghost.

"Caleb, I—"

"Please, just hear me out." He stepped into her space, his aura flickering with emotion, the sorrow in his eyes deepening. "It's more important than you realize. You've come so far, but there's more left to uncover. I can't find peace without you understanding what happened. You need to find me … where I am."

Riley nodded slowly, her heart aching for the pain he carried. "I know a bit about the rivalry you had, but I don't know everything. I want to help you."

Caleb's gaze softened as he took a breath, the movement gentle yet charged with urgency. "I didn't just lose my life that night; I lost everything I had dreamed of. I wanted to be a counselor, to connect with campers, to inspire them. My dreams didn't have to die with me. They lived on, trapped here, waiting for someone to acknowledge them."

His words stabbed at her heart, amplifying her own longing. She had her dreams too—plans for her future, friendships blooming beautifully, and a connection with Ethan that felt warm and bright. But standing here with Caleb reminded her of the ties that bound her to both the living and the dead.

Caleb continued, his voice trembling with intensity. "I need you to find me. My life was stolen from me, and it's not just my burden; it's yours now too. The shadows here won't let you move on until you help me set me free."

"Can you give me a clue?" Riley asked, feeling the urgency.

Caleb turned his head away from her, "Look in the woods. Hidden in branches, out of sight. A whispered secret, a quiet place, a peaceful haven, a hidden space."

A quiet place? A hidden space? Riley was perplexed. That sounded like a riddle! She met his gaze, and in that moment, the lines between their worlds blurred—all the pain, the fear, and the hope coalescing into an undeniable force. She felt genuinely connected to his plight in a way she never had before.

But then, just as those thoughts swirled through her mind, she felt a warmth behind her. Turning slowly, Riley saw Ethan approaching, a wide smile that illuminated his already attractive features. He exuded confidence, confidence that unnerved her during this already tense moment with Caleb.

"Hey, I was looking for you." Ethan glanced around, his expression shifting as he perceived the heavy air surrounding Riley and Caleb. His smile faded, replaced by a hint of concern. "Is everything okay?"

Riley's heartbeat raced as she felt the heaviness of her dual existence, the tension between the comforting pull of her feelings for Ethan and the urgent longing that stirred in the presence of Caleb. She wanted to plunge deeper into Caleb's world, to uncover the mystery for him, but how could she turn her back on Ethan?

She turned back to Caleb, seeking affirmation, but his pleading eyes sought her own, asking for her commitment. "Riley, find me," Caleb said, his voice barely above a whisper yet carrying its own weight.

Ethan's brow furrowed slightly. "What's going on? You look... I don't know—distracted." He stepped closer, sensing her emotional turmoil.

Riley felt rooted in place, trapped between two worlds. "Ethan, I've been given a clue as to where we can find him," she said, words choked with emotion. Her heart felt like it was splintering with each passing second.

Caleb stood just a breath away, his presence a shrouded promise of understanding yet laden with unsaid words. The world felt suspended; her heart raced, thrumming against her ribs with uncertainty.

Ethan's gaze darted between her and dead air—confusion flashing across his face. "Riley, talk to me. What do you mean?"

Riley drew in a steadying breath as Caleb's ethereal form flickered beside her, his eyes pleading with an urgency that stirred her soul. She turned to Ethan, knowing she needed to share the revelation Caleb had entrusted her with.

"He gave me a riddle," she began, her voice wavering slightly. "Caleb said that to find him, to help him find peace, I need to look in the woods. He said, 'hidden in branches, out of sight. A peaceful haven, a hidden space.'"

Ethan's brow furrowed as he processed her words, and for a moment, disbelief flickered across his features. Riley braced herself for the skepticism she had grown accustomed to from others, but Ethan surprised her.

"When Caleb first went missing back in 1975, there was an extensive search of the surrounding woods," he said, his voice low and contemplative. "The camp staff and local authorities combed through every inch of these grounds, but they never found a trace of him."

Riley felt a flicker of hope ignite within her. "So there are records of that search? Logs or maps they used?"

Ethan nodded, his expression growing more resolute. "Yeah, they're stored in the camp office. If we can get our hands on those documents, we might be able to devise a plan—a fresh set of eyes on the same area."

A sense of purpose surged through Riley as she realized the opportunity before them. With Ethan's support and the potential clues from the past search efforts, they had a chance to unravel the mystery that had eluded so many.

"We should review those logs," she said, her voice gaining strength. "If we can create a grid search pattern based on the areas they covered, we might be able to find something they missed."

Ethan's expression softened, and he reached out, squeezing her shoulder reassuringly. "I'm with you on this, Riley. But..." He hesitated, and a hint of concern flickered in his eyes. "We don't have much time left here. The camp session is almost over, and all the campers will be heading home in a few days."

Riley felt her heart sink at the reminder of their limited window. She had become so consumed by her quest to help Caleb that she had momentarily forgotten the looming reality of their impending departure.

"Ethan, I know it seems impossible," she said, her voice laced with determination. "If trained professionals couldn't find him back then, how can we hope to succeed now? But I have to try. Caleb's spirit is counting on me, and I can't just abandon him."

Ethan studied her for a moment, his gaze intense and searching. Finally, he nodded, a small smile tugging at the corners of his mouth. "Okay, then we'll give it our best shot. Let's get our hands on those logs and start planning our search."

Relief washed over Riley, and she felt a surge of gratitude for Ethan's unwavering support. With him by her side, she knew they had a fighting chance to uncover the truth and bring Caleb the closure he so desperately sought.

As they turned and made their way back towards the camp office, Riley cast one last glance over her shoulder, half-expecting to see Caleb's ghostly form lingering nearby. But the shoreline was empty, save for the gentle lapping of waves against the rocky shore. Still, she could sense his presence, a silent encouragement urging her forward on this path—a path that would test her resolve and her heart in ways she could never have imagined.

what's in the riddle

Morning sunlight filtered through the camp office windows, illuminating layers of dust coating old wooden desks. Riley and Ethan rifled through weathered files and bound logbooks, their hearts pounding with the anticipation of discovery. The air buzzed with a mix of excitement and trepidation as memories of Caleb's tragic past filled their minds.

"Look at this!" Ethan's voice cut through the silence, and Riley leaned in closer, her breath hitching as he pointed to a faded photograph. It depicted a cheerful group of camp counselors, all smiles and sunshine, Caleb standing proudly among them with a confident grin. Yet, beneath the festive exterior, an eerie aura loomed—the thought of the kindness stripped away far too soon, leaving only unanswered questions.

"Here," he continued, flipping through pages with an urgency that matched her own. Riley braced herself for shocking revelations, searching through musty pages that whispered tales of the camp's past.

Finally, Ethan found what they'd been looking for: a neatly penciled entry about the day Caleb went missing in 1975.

"The search discovered no signs of Caleb. Limited visibility due to dense foliage and echoes of laughter impeded early attempts," he read aloud, his voice low yet steady, "but members of the community reported whispers of strange noises… sightings of a flickering lantern that led us deeper into the woods."

"Gawd, no wonder everyone gave up! What kind of search is that?"

"They weren't as sophisticated as we are back then. We have cell phones, and technology they never have," Ethan chimed.

Riley's spirit raced with a blend of dread and determination as she absorbed the written words. Those echoes of laughter that had seemed innocent decades ago were now infused with tragedy. Nothing would stop her from uncovering the truth behind Caleb's past.

Across the table, she saw Ethan's brow furrow, his concentration unyielding. "This makes everything feel… real. We have to figure out how to help him."

"Are you ready to do this?" she asked, the gravity of the moment piercing through their shared elation. They needed to find closure—not just for Caleb, but for themselves.

With the dawning light of a new day, Riley, Ethan, and their closest friends assembled near the campsite. They packed their backpacks with water, snacks, and flashlights, their hearts tuning into the rhythm of the approaching adventure. Surrounded by laughter and nervous chatter, Riley felt the weight of expectation settle around her shoulders—hers and Caleb's.

"Okay, let's hit the forest!" Ethan announced, adjusting the straps on his backpack. As they moved into the trees, sunlight flickered through the dense foliage. The world fell quiet, save for the rustling of leaves and the crunching of twigs beneath their feet.

As they trekked deeper into the woods, Riley's mind buzzed with the words she had memorized.

"Hidden in branches, out of sight. A whispered secret, a quiet place, a peaceful haven, a hidden space."

The riddle echoed in her thoughts, leading her forward, a melody coaxed by the ghosts of the past. Answers danced just beyond reach, but doubts lingered. *Would they find him? Would it be too late?* A chill raced down her spine, but she fought against it, focusing instead on each step.

"Riley!" Ethan called, his voice harmonizing with the

distant call of the forest. "What do you think that riddle means?"

"I… I think it's something we'll know when we see it—an old tree, maybe?" She felt a spark ignite within her. "We have to keep looking. He wants us to find him."

Every bush brushed against her arms, the scent of damp earth filling her lungs as the group pressed on, hearts drumming excitedly at the prospect of what lay ahead.

Hours unraveled like threads, the sun shifting overhead as the towering trees cloaked them in shadows. They paused to catch their breath, taking sips from their water bottles before pushing onward.

Suddenly, a cool breeze swept through the woods, carrying with it a hint of something familiar. Riley felt it, that electric tingle, just like when Caleb appeared to her before. She looked around, straining to feel his presence in the whispering leaves and the delicate rustling above.

"Riley," a voice floated to her through the thickening air. It was soft, almost imperceptible, and yet it ignited her determination. "Follow me."

She stepped forward, drawn away from the group, feeling an invisible tether pulling her deeper into the wild. Ethan noticed Riley's departure and followed closely, concern etched into his features.

"Riley, wait!"

But her feet moved with a purpose, each step bringing Caleb's ethereal voice into sharper focus. The forest opened up to a clearing, revealing a tall, ancient tree standing sentinel over an unseen secret. Its gnarled branches reached for the sky, the bark worn and weathered like an old friend.

"Caleb?" she whispered, heart racing.

"Look," Ethan urged, tilting his head in the direction she was facing.

Riley watched as Caleb's translucent figure flickered into view, positioned beside the mighty tree. He appeared calm, gentler than before, and a warm glow radiated from him, illuminating their surroundings.

Her breath caught. *Was this truly it?*

"Hidden in branches," Caleb echoed softly, guiding her gaze upward. "To find peace, seek the truth."

Riley gazed up, and a lump formed in her throat. "What do you mean?"

He left her with a tender smile before gesturing to the heights of the tree. "Climb, Riley. A hidden space awaits..."

The whispers of the leaves and branches seemed to support her as she clung to the sturdy trunk, climbing higher with Ethan close behind. As she reached the first set of thick branches, a sudden flutter of wind brushed against her cheek, like a gentle reminder from Caleb.

Finally, at the top, Riley pointed her binoculars into the distance, widening her eyes in disbelief. Hidden from view, entwined within the branches, skeletal remains were bound to the trunk. Her heart sank as she processed the sight of twisted bones, trapped in a grim sleep.

"Oh gawd—Caleb," she cried, unable to suppress the emotions flooding through her.

Caleb's presence surged around her, his expression tranquil yet full of gratitude. He beamed at Riley as if she were his guiding light, the one who had finally brought an end to his restless wandering.

"Thank you," he whispered, echoing as if it were carried away by the wind.

Tears streamed down Riley's cheeks—angelic and heavy with sorrow. She felt the enormity of the moment, the pain, and the fragility of the life he had lost. Unable to articulate her feelings, she nodded, a deep sense of peace washing over her, knowing they had finally solved the riddle of his disappearance.

13
the ritual of release

The sky darkened, shades of purple and blue swirling together as the sun dipped below the horizon. Dusk settled over Camp Willowood like a thick blanket, and shadows elongated beneath the towering pine trees. The atmosphere hummed with an electric tension, heightened by the flickering candles Riley and her friends were busy arranging in a secluded glade.

"Okay, we've got most of what we need," Riley said, kneeling on the ground and placing a bundle of wildflowers she'd picked earlier near the makeshift altar they'd formed with logs and stones. Each flower held significance—lilies for purity, daisies for innocence, and a few cheerful sunflowers to represent the light and hope they wished for Caleb.

"Are you sure this is going to work?" Emily asked, rummaging through her backpack for the small bundle of charms she had crafted. Her breath was slightly shaky, betraying her skepticism. "What if it doesn't? Or worse, what if we accidentally open a portal or something?"

Riley secured her gaze on Emily, a hint of annoyance mixing with empathy. "We're not summoning demons, Em. This is for Caleb. He deserves this."

"As if he isn't already trapped in some sort of ghostly purgatory," Emily muttered, but there was a reluctant understanding in her eyes.

They all felt it—the gravity of what they were about to do. Riley pushed aside her own apprehensions. She could feel Caleb's presence, a growing ache in her heart that urged them forward. It was time to release him from the bonds of his past.

Ethan knelt opposite Riley, his brow furrowed as he flicked a glance toward the darkening woods. "I just— I want to be sure we know what we're doing," he admitted, brushing a hand through his tousled hair. "Rituals can backfire. This isn't a game."

Riley met his gaze, and in the dim light, the intensity of his blue eyes darkened with concern. She held herself steady, but something inside twisted—a flicker of doubt.

"It's okay to be scared," she said, her voice softening. "But we can't let fear hold us back. We owe it to Caleb."

Ethan nodded but stayed silent, his demeanor betraying worry. He was leaning into her, supporting her choices, but the bond deepened with every word left unsaid.

As they continued to gather items, Riley turned her attention to Jake, who had been unusually quiet. He approached with a small, old photograph he had discovered in his cabin—a faded image of Caleb laughing, surrounded by campers.

"Check this out," Jake muttered, giving Emily a side-eye. "Snagged it from my cabin, tucked away in some old drawer. Figure it might do us some good, y'know?" He set the worn-out picture beside the flowers with care.

Riley felt a pang in her chest. She wanted to know more about Caleb's life—the laughter, the friendships he had woven into the fabric of Camp Willowood.

The air around them felt thick with anticipation as the last of the daylight faded away, casting the glade in muted twilight. The shadows danced, twisting through spaces, and Riley felt the gentle caress of a soft breeze brush against her skin, almost as if Caleb were there with them.

"Okay, I think we have everything," she said, trying to stow the weight of doubt creeping at the corners of her mind. "We should draw a circle and get started."

As Riley moved to create a symbol in the dirt beneath her, the others chimed in with murmurs of encouragement, though their eyes betrayed their unease. She spoke softly under her breath, inspiring courage into the circle they began forming.

While Riley worked, Ethan stepped closer, hovering just outside the circle. "Are you sure we should do this alone? Maybe we could get someone with more experience involved?"

"I can feel him," she replied, her voice firm but laced with the tremors of her own uncertainty. "We've come this far. I can't back out now. This is the best chance we have to help him."

Ethan's expression softened, but the knot in his brow remained.

"Fine," he said, his tone less authoritative, carrying an undeniable warmth. "Just... be careful. You mean a lot to me."

Riley's heart fluttered, as she felt both gratitude and guilt tightening her chest. She turned back to the gathered group, busily arranging candles and flowers. There was something about preparing for this ritual that felt almost sacred—the collective energy of her friends came together, intertwining hopes for Caleb while honing their focus on their intentions. This felt vast and monumental—a responsibility that rested heavily on her shoulders.

"Let's light the candles," Riley declared. She lit each one carefully, offering a prayer in silence for Caleb's peace, curling her fingers around the flickering flames to breathe life into their intentions.

The glow illuminated their faces, a mix of determination and anxiety. As the last candle sparkled to life, a sudden chill wrapped around them uninvited, whispers brushing against their ears. They all exchanged glances, a sudden awareness dawning—a shared recognition of the unknown territory they were about to step into.

"Did you feel that?" Riley's voice wavered, her heart racing as she met Ethan's gaze. The flame of the candles danced erratically as if stirred by an unseen wind.

Steve's eyes were wide. "It's just the wind," he said, but there was uncertainty beneath his bravado.

Riley pressed her lips together, forcing her mind to clear the whirlpool of doubt. She smiled, determined to keep the focus as exhilaration bubbled inside her. "Let's finish setting up our offerings. He needs to know we care."

They arranged the photo, flowers, and small trinkets—everything taking on a life of its own, weaving threads of meaning through the gathering dusk. With every careful placement, Riley felt more entwined with Caleb's spirit and what he might have meant to Camp Willowood.

But a sudden rustle in the nearby bushes made their hearts leap. Riley glanced towards the sound, and for a moment, her resolve wavered. The uncertainty loomed over the group like an ominous storm cloud, threatening to scatter their purpose into the unknown.

"No turning back now," Ethan murmured beside her, and she felt the warmth of his presence, grounding her as fear briefly clouded her determination.

"We've come too far," Riley echoed, her conviction returning like a flame reignited. The combination of duty and hope pushed them forward, a collective drive bolstered by Caleb's haunting shadows blending into their own lives.

As dusk transitioned into a velvet night, the stars blinked overhead, and they felt Caleb's spirit encircle them—a protective embrace urging them to carry on. Riley closed her eyes, focusing on the warmth of the candles, and the first uncertainties melted away.

With everyone ready, Riley kept her voice steady. "Let's do this for him."

* * *

RILEY'S HANDS TREMBLED SLIGHTLY, a mix of exhilaration and trepidation coursing through her. She could feel the weight of her friends' eyes on her, filled with expectation and a touch of disbelief. The clearing was aglow with white candles, their flames flickering softly in the cool night breeze, throwing playful shadows against the trees. Riley stepped into the circle, heart pounding as she arranged the candles into a perfect pattern, breathing in the earthy scent of the woods mixed with floral undertones.

"Is this really going to work?" Emily whispered, her brow furrowed with concern. The others murmured their uncertainties, each glancing around nervously. But Riley had to believe.

"Trust me, we've come this far. It has to," Riley replied, her voice steady as she faced her friends. They all shared a mix of fear and excitement but, beneath it all, a shared belief that they needed to do this for Caleb.

Once satisfied with their setup, Riley drew a deep breath, inhaling the fresh, pine-scented air, the night charged with energy. She focused on the task at hand, letting go of the doubts that threatened to creep back in. She recalled the incantation she'd memorized, words that echoed from the pages of an old book she found tucked within the yellowing newspapers. This was no longer just a story—this was about Caleb, and his freedom.

"Everyone, hold hands," Riley instructed, feeling their fingers interlock around her own, a solid chain of support. They formed a circle, their connected camaraderie amplifying the energy coiling around them. "We'll start together."

With a shaky yet determined voice, Riley began to chant the incantation.

"O spirit bound by grief and fate, we call upon you to release this weight. Rise up to the sky where your soul may roam, find your peace and journey home."

As she spoke, her friends joined in, their voices blending into a rhythmic chorus that echoed through the trees. With every word, Riley felt a shift in the air around them, a thrumming sensation beneath her skin as the moonlight intensified, illuminating the clearing like a soft spotlight. The flickering flames flickered wildly, as if responding to their invocation.

Caleb's presence began to solidify before them, shimmering at the edge of the circle, his ethereal glow brighter under the night sky. He hovered there, transient and haunting; his sorrowful eyes determined yet filled with an unbearable weight. For a moment, he seemed almost tangible, as if he had stepped beyond the veil just for them.

"Caleb," Riley whispered, her heart swelling with emotion. His figure flickered but stabilized as he met her gaze, her voice breaking through the shared silence.

Caleb's expression shifted, a mixture of raw longing and gratitude shining in his eyes. He reached out, his hand grazing the edge of the light cast by the candles, creating ripples of energy, a sigh in the air that whispered secrets none could fully comprehend.

The chants ebbed for a moment as they observed him, their connection strengthening. A soft breeze swept through the clearing, swirling the petals of the flowers and illuminating Caleb's face, revealing the vulnerability within him.

With a sudden breath, Riley resumed the incantation, pushing herself into the rhythm. "We gather here as friends of the past, offering our light for your spirit to last. Let go of the ties that hold you so near, find peace in our hearts and release all your fear."

As their voices rose, Caleb's essence brightened, flickering more vibrantly. He nodded slowly, a tear glistening in his ghostly eye, and for a moment, Riley felt a wave of warmth wash over her, intertwining their souls in a fleeting embrace. His emotions flooded into her, a powerful rush that held both the weight of his sorrow and the glimmer of promise.

But as the energy swelled around them, Riley sensed something amiss. A cold rush of air whipped through the clearing, extinguishing a few of the candles. Shadows deepened in the surrounding trees, and a subtle tension began to weave through the atmosphere like a silken thread.

"What's happening?" one of her friends whispered, unease lacing their voice.

Riley clenched her jaw but kept her focus on Caleb. "We can do this. Just… stay connected."

As if on cue, a soft wail twisted through the air, slicing the moment of connection. It echoed around them, a haunting reminder of the unresolved pain in Caleb's heart, heavier than the darkness that surrounded the camp. He flinched, his form flickering again, caught between worlds, struggling against the chains that bound him.

"Caleb, look at me!" Riley exclaimed, desperation seeping into her voice. "You have to fight this. We're here for you!"

Understanding flickered in his eyes as their gazes locked once more. She felt a surge of warmth course through her hand, the grip of her friends linking them together.

"Caleb, you're not alone." Riley reaffirmed, her voice gaining strength as she pushed through the fear clutching at her heart. "You can let go. We believe in you."

With renewed conviction, she led her friends back into the incantation, voices intertwining like threads of fate. "We gather here to release your pain, to honor your spirit, and break every chain."

The clearing began to vibrate with energy, pulses of warmth radiating from the circle, wrapping around Caleb and urging him to find the light once more. But just as hope blossomed, Caleb's form shifted with confusion, an unseen force pulling him in disparate directions.

Riley's heart raced, sensing the profound struggle within him. For a fleeting moment, doubts crept into her mind— was this truly going to help, or would it only deepen the chaos? Yet, she couldn't back down now.

"Caleb, you're free now, go now—go towards the light!"

Her voice rang with conviction, drowning out the darkness that threatened to overwhelm them.

* * *

"YOU'VE SUFFERED LONG ENOUGH. It's okay to let go. You're not alone. We're all here with you," she said, her words spilling from her heart. Around her, the group tightened their grip on each other, their fingers interlaced, channeling their collective energy towards Caleb. They could feel the weight of his unrest, the remnants of a life interrupted.

For a moment, silence reigned in the clearing, the only sounds the rhythmic waves of breath from Riley and her friends. Caleb's form flickered again, shimmering like sunlight on water, yet he remained still—for how long, Riley couldn't tell. She sensed the battle within him: the overwhelming urge to cling to the past juxtaposed against a burgeoning desire for freedom.

"Remember your friends, Caleb," she implored, tears prickling the corners of her eyes. "Remember the laughter, the joys. Don't let the shadows take that away from you."

His eyes widened, reflecting fleeting memories, echoes of laughter, and sun-drenched days at Camp Willowood. Riley felt a rush of warmth, recognizing that the spirit she spoke to was more than a mere specter; he was a boy who had lived, loved, and dreamed.

A gust of wind swept through the clearing, drawing with it the scent of pine and earth, its howling echoing the tumult of Caleb's heart. The flickering flames of the candles sputtered out wildly, plunging them into brief darkness before Riley, instinctively, reignited the candles with her willpower, refusing to yield to chaos.

Beyond the candlelight, shadows swirled as Caleb's form trembled, the ghostly aura contorting in emotional strife. He seemed to waver, flickering like a candle barely holding onto its flame.

Riley took a step closer, feeling the draw of his presence; she could almost feel the warmth emanating from him, like the last breaths of a dying fire. "It's time, Caleb. Don't be afraid. You've got to choose to move on. You have to confront what happened. We're all supporting you."

Within the depths of Caleb's eyes, a flicker of understanding sparked, as if her words were slowly permeating the walls he had built around his heart. A moment of stillness enveloped them, the world outside fading into oblivion—the only existence was the three of them, connected in this fragile moment.

With a gentle nod, Caleb's form fluctuated, and Riley felt a surge of power radiate through her friends, their hands squeezing tighter as they sent their collective warmth and love to him. More voices joined Riley's, her friends echoing her sentiments, enveloping Caleb with encouragement.

He hesitated, the tension palpable, and Riley felt a tear slip down her cheek. "Let yourself be free, Caleb. Find the peace you deserve," she whispered urgently, locking eyes with him. "It's okay. We'll be with you, spirit with soul, forever."

The atmosphere shifted, a profound moment of clarity dawning on Caleb. He took a deep breath, or at least Riley imagined he did, as a bright light began to emanate from him. It radiated warmth that enveloped the clearing, washing over them and filling Riley with a sense of comfort. This was it—his moment of release.

As Caleb's form began to shimmer and fade, Riley felt a bittersweet ache in her heart; the connection they had forged, so unique and tender, hung heavy in the air. A final flash of emotion crossed Caleb's face, a mixture of sorrow for the past and joy for the future. Bright, brilliant light embraced him fully, engulfing the space in a golden glow.

Riley squeezed her friends' hands tighter, her heart racing, every nerve ending vibrating with the weight of what was unfolding. "Goodbye, Caleb," she breathed, her voice a mere whisper against the luminous backdrop.

Caleb's eyes glistened with tears as the light surrounded him. Just before he faded completely, he mouthed a silent thank you, a farewell that transcended words. The air shimmered one last time as he disappeared into the ether, leaving behind an echo of warmth that reverberated through the gathering.

The clearing fell silent. The candles extinguished on their own as though washed clean by the light of Caleb's release. Alone, yet surrounded by her friends, Riley stared into the empty space where he had been, the silence reverberating in her heart. A profound sense of loss settled within her, a bittersweet yearning mixed with overwhelming gratitude.

She still felt the gentle brush of his spirit against her consciousness, the bond shared, both tangible and ethereal. As she looked around at her friends, their eyes reflected the same understanding—the weight of the moment pressed against each of them, a lasting connection forged not just with Caleb but with each other.

Riley closed her eyes, inhaling deeply, feeling every pulse of the summer night. She opened her eyes, letting the soft moonlight embrace her, cherishing the bond they shared while looking toward her future, one forever touched by a love that would remain etched in her heart.

14
farewell to the past

The first light of dawn crept over Camp Willowood, casting a gentle glow upon the crystalline lake. Soft whispers of emerald-hued pines stirred in the morning breeze, and birds began their joyful symphony. The air hung delicately with the scent of dew-kissed grass and distant campfires, remnants of last night's gathering still lingering like memories in the cool air.

Riley sat cross-legged on the edge of the lake, the water rippling in synchrony with her thoughts. She hugged her knees close to her chest, feeling the warmth from the sun slowly replacing the chill of night with a golden embrace. She still could hardly process the whirlwind of emotions from the ritual; it whipped around her like the gentle waves lapping at the shore.

How had it come to this? Just a few weeks ago, Riley had arrived at Camp Willowood, nerves tingling at the thought of spending her final summer before senior year among so many strangers. Now, the camp felt like a second home, a sanctuary filled with laughter, friendships, and—most haunting of all—an unforgettable connection with Caleb Whitaker. The whole experience had shifted something deep within her, awakening parts of her heart she hadn't known were dormant.

Riley's mind drifted back to the night of the ritual, to the moment when Caleb's radiant form faded away. The way his eyes had reflected both sorrow and relief, the energy that had crackled in the air—it was as if she had caught a glimpse of the soul's essence. They had shared something profound, something that transcended the limitations of life and death. Even now, a bittersweet heaviness settled in her chest at the thought of saying goodbye.

Yet the fond memories of their time together mingled with heartache. Riley smiled through her sorrow, recalling his selfless nature, the unyielding determination he carried even in the spectral realm. Caleb's spirit had been brave, revealing snippets of his life and the weight of his lost dreams. Each revelation had drawn her closer, merging her life with his— two disparate souls joined by remnants of time and unspoken words.

As she looked at the water, a flower fell from her pocket and landed on the grass next to her. It was a single blossom, the one she had taken as a souvenir from the ritual: a wildflower picked from the meadow, bright yet withering, a reminder of the beauty and fragility of life. Its petals, once vibrant, were starting to curl at the edges, a sign of the impermanence of all things. She carefully picked it up again, holding it in front of her as if it were precious.

This flower symbolized so much more than just a physical connection to what had transpired; it was a tangible reminder of closure and memory. Caleb's departure hadn't just been a farewell; it had been a releasement, a bittersweet acknowledgment of his importance in her life. Riley finally accepted that it was time to carry forward, to take the lessons she had learned and let them guide her as she walked away from the shadows of the past.

"Everything is a cycle," she murmured to the ribbon of water before her. "Time to make room for what's next."

In the distance, the camp began to stir awake. Laughter and chatter floated lightly over the stillness of the lake, a reminder of the lively day ahead. Riley gathered herself, rising to her feet. The brilliance of the morning light teetered between warmth and chill, much like the ambivalence swirling within her heart. Standing atop the land where life thrived, she felt both the weight of Caleb's memory and the excitement for new beginnings.

With each step toward the cabins, Riley was consumed with thoughts of her friends and Ethan. Her heart fluttered at the recollection of late-night conversations filled with laughter, secrets shared around the campfire, and the magnetic warmth in Ethan's presence. He had been the sun to her moon, lighting up the night when she felt lost in her thoughts. His laughter brought a melody to her summer that she couldn't overlook.

But the tingling sensation at the back of her mind was persistent, a reminder of a promise she had made to Caleb. To not only cherish the past but also to embrace what lay before her. She could not let the story end on such a note; she needed to honor his memory by ensuring that his essence lived on through her actions, through the connections she formed with others.

Riley carefully tucked the wilted flower in her braid, a silent vow to hold onto the lessons of compassion, understanding, and bravery she had learned. As she approached her cabin, the sights and sounds of camp filled her with hope, allowing healing to seep gently into her heart. She longed to share her journey with her friends, to convey the complexities of what she had experienced—the joy found in Caleb's presence, the ache of letting go, and the vibrant possibilities waiting just beyond.

With each breath, she felt the heavy fog of anxiety lift, replaced with clarity. She was ready to embrace the future, step into the collective experiences of friendship, and allow herself to love again.

The sun climbed higher in the sky, illuminating the path before her with warmth and vibrancy. In this serene moment, she made a silent promise, not just to Caleb but to herself—to live fully and without reservation, to explore the depths of her heart while nurturing those connections that filled her world with light.

As she stepped back toward the gathering with newfound conviction, she knew the memory of Caleb would always accompany her like a protective shadow. It was a part of her story, a precious chapter that had changed everything, and as she walked with purpose, a thought glimmered bright in her mind. She would become the person she was meant to be, blossoming like the flowers covering the meadow, leaving behind a legacy worth remembering.

THE LAST DAY at Camp Willowood dawned bright and clear, the warm sun stretching over the treetops and casting long shadows on the lawn where campers gathered. Laughter and chatter filled the air, mingling with the smell of breakfast wafting from the dining hall. Riley felt a swell of nostalgia wash over her as she joined her friends, heading towards the central clearing where the final assembly was held.

The annual tradition of recounting memories was a cherished highlight, a bittersweet moment of celebration interwoven with sadness. Campers spilled into the space, exchanging hugs, and wildflowers from the surrounding fields were braided into hair, wreaths, and bracelets as a symbol of their shared experiences.

As Riley took her place among her cabinmates, a palpable sense of anticipation buzzed in the air. She glanced around at the familiar faces, their expressions a mix of excitement and melancholy. They settled onto the grass in a haphazard circle, eager to share their stories.

"Okay, who wants to kick things off?" Ethan asked, his warm smile radiating positivity. He leaned back on his hands, exuding the calm confidence that drew Riley in all summer long.

"I'm starting!" Emily declared, plopping down next to Riley. "Remember the canoe race? You guys totally cheated!" Laughter erupted, echoing through the clearing as Riley feigned offense.

"Cheated? We simply knew how to paddle better!" Riley retorted playfully, nudging Emily with her shoulder.

As the stories continued, each camper shared a memory that encapsulated a moment of joy, a mishap, or a lesson learned. Riley's heart swelled with each recounting, recognizing the warmth of camaraderie that had blossomed over the summer.

"Riley," Jake spoke up after he had finished sharing about the spooky night hike, "you were so determined to get to the bottom of that Caleb mystery. I'm really proud of you. You led us all to something incredible."

Riley's face flushed as she smiled. "Thanks, Jake. I couldn't have done it without you guys," she replied, her voice full of sincerity. "You all played a part in this. It wasn't just me. It was our shared journey."

The mood shifted warmly, enveloping the group in a blanket of gratitude. Each friend expressed their appreciation for Riley's leadership, their voices tinged with emotions that mirrored her own. The acknowledgment felt like a balm to her growing sense of loss, both for Caleb and the friendships that had blossomed yet were about to fade.

As the day wore on, the excitement blended with nostalgia, each activity a reminder of the fleeting time they had spent together. They explored the lake, leather bracelets wrinkled from their sun-kissed skin, played games with the younger campers and found solace in the knowledge that their memories were etched forever in the heart of the camp.

The sun began to dip low in the sky, casting hues of orange and pink across the horizon. Riley felt her heart tighten at the thought of parting ways from this experience, and more importantly, from the friends who had witnessed her journey. It was time for the final moment of goodbyes.

As the evening approached, the group convened around the campfire. Flickering flames danced in the night, illuminating their faces, casting shadows that whispered stories of summer adventures. Riley felt a lump in her throat as she prepared to embrace the inevitable goodbyes.

"I'm going to miss this place," Emily said softly, leaning against Riley. "And you, Riles. I don't think I've ever made a friend quite like you."

"Right back at you," Riley replied, blinking back hot tears. "This summer changed me. I'll carry all of you with me, always."

One by one, they exchanged promises of texting and video calls, each vow imbued with a hope that their experiences wouldn't just evaporate with the summer sun.

Ethan moved closer, wrapping an arm around Riley's shoulders and pulling her slightly away from the group, creating a private pocket amidst the crowd. He had that serious yet gentle expression she had grown accustomed to —the one that made her heart race with uncertainty.

"Riley," Ethan began, his voice low, yet firm. "I know we're all leaving tomorrow, but...I wanted you to know how much I care about you." He paused, searching her eyes for understanding. "I didn't expect to feel this way, but..."

"Ethan..." Riley's heart raced as she seized the moment to confront the true depth of her feelings, but fear of what that might lead to held her back.

"Let me finish," he urged, his face earnest. "I'm not saying this just because camp is ending. I mean it. You've changed my perspective on everything, and I don't want just memories. I want a future, Riley."

His confession hung in the air, charging the space between them with a tension that held her breath captive. She wanted to respond, to reassure him, but part of her felt tied to the past—both with Caleb's lingering shadow and her own insecurities about what life beyond camp held.

"And I want that too," Riley managed, feeling a knot form in her chest. "But… I'm not sure how this works. After camp, everything changes."

Ethan stepped a fraction closer, the warmth of his presence wrapping around her, making the other concerns fade for a moment. "We can figure it out together. I don't want to lose what we have because of distance. Let's stay connected."

The vulnerability in his voice stirred something deep within Riley. She appreciated how he was willing to weather the unknown alongside her, understanding her hesitations and internal struggles.

"You really mean that?" Riley whispered, searching his face for any sign of uncertainty.

"More than anything." He smiled softly, brushing a stray hair behind her ear.

Somewhere in her heart, the icy tendrils of fear began to thaw as hope sparked—perhaps the threads binding them together all summer could follow them into the unknown.

In that charged moment, the crackle of the campfire was the only sound that filled the air—a testament to the shared history and yet uncharted future that awaited them. They stood poised at the precipice of change, ready to take the plunge together, their hearts beating in harmony under the vast, starry sky.

Just as Riley opened her mouth to respond, the clamoring voices of their friends beckoned them back into the circle, laughter spilling over. They drifted back to the group, warmth still lingering in the space between them, a shared promise hanging delicately in the air, unwilling to be put to rest.

* * *

AS THE SUN dipped behind the trees, casting shimmering reflections on the surface of the lake, Riley found herself slipping away from the chaos of Camp Willowood one last time. The air was thick with bittersweet nostalgia; campers chatted excitedly as they awaited their buses, some reliving shared memories over the past couple of weeks. But Riley needed solitude—the kind that allowed her to breathe, to reconnect with the tender ache in her heart.

She stepped softly toward the lakeside, feeling the cool grass under her bare feet. Each step brought back echoes of laughter, whispers of secrets shared with both her friends and the ghost that had so profoundly changed her summer. The lake's surface waved gently, the water lapping softly against the shore as if inviting her into its embrace.

Sitting at the water's edge, she gazed into the shimmering depths, allowing herself to drift into thought. The vibrant memories swirled in her mind. Caleb's playful antics, the moments they shared under the stars, and the weight of his sorrow mixed with the warmth he brought to her life. She felt a lightness now, the heaviness of grief lifting just enough to make room for gratitude.

"Caleb," she whispered, her voice barely more than a breath against the shimmering surface. "Thank you for everything. You... you showed me what it means to care deeply, to connect."

She thought back to the last night, the ritual, how Caleb had shown her not just his pain, but the beauty of life he had lost—his laughter, the joy he brought to campers, and the way he had once relished every moment. As she reflected on their shared journey, a warmth enveloped her, tinged with sadness yet also with a profound sense of peace.

"Goodbye… for now," she said, her voice trembling slightly. A flutter of wind danced through the trees, rustling the leaves with a soft sigh, as if nature itself had heard her farewell.

Then it happened—a faint rustle nearby, followed by a gentle illumination. Caleb's spirit materialized beside her, his ghostly figure shimmering with an ethereal glow that seemed softer, more serene than before. He appeared lighter, free from the sorrow that had once marked his celestial form. It struck her how magnificent he looked, the moonlight cascading down like a silver blanket, emphasizing the delicate features of a boy untouched by time.

Riley gasped, air catching in her throat.

"Caleb," she breathed, her heart racing with a mix of joy and disbelief.

A soft smile crossed Caleb's face—a smile that radiated warmth, filled with gratitude. His eyes, once sorrowful, glistened with a sense of calmness that assured her he had found peace. He gestured toward the lake, then placed a hand over his heart, expressing emotions more profound than words.

"I… I didn't expect to see you again," she said, attempting to steady her voice. The sight of him stirred a tide of emotions; her heart swelled with connections and memories they shared, with what he meant to her.

Caleb nodded slowly, his expression filled with kindness. In that silent moment, they understood each other—the space between them charged with the echoes of everything left unsaid yet deeply felt.

"Thank you for helping me find closure," his voice echoed softly, peeling back layers of lingering sorrow that had woven themselves around her heart. With each word, she felt his gratitude wrap around her like a warm embrace.

"I wish—" she started, but the words faltered. Her mind rushed to the uncertainty of their connection, the impossibility of crossing the boundary between worlds. Yet, she realized there was no need for those wishes. He had shown her so much, had opened her heart in ways she never expected.

Caleb tilted his head slightly, a gesture of reassurance as though he read her heart as easily as the gentle ripples on the lake. He stepped closer, ethereal light radiating from him, making the world around them brighter, softer.

"Remember me," he urged, the sorrow gone from his tone, replaced with the resonance of hope. "Hold onto the moments we shared, and live freely, Riley."

Tears brimmed in her eyes, each drop a precious memory of their journey together. Their bond transcended everything, even death, but she still found herself aching with the inevitability of parting.

"I will never forget you," she promised, voice shaking as she took in every detail of his radiant form—the soft waves of his hair, the gentle curve of his smile. "You've changed my life forever."

A hint of sadness flickered across Caleb's expression. He raised his hand, almost reaching out, and for just a moment, Riley felt an electric connection, the undeniable bond that had grown between them during their brief time together.

"The stars will guide you," he said, his gaze unwavering on hers, filled with an ancient wisdom that transcended the confines of time. "In every night's sky, I'll be with you."

The words echoed in her heart, and in that moment, she understood the enormity of their connection. She would carry him forward in her heart, a piece of his spirit intertwining with her own.

As if sensing the impermanence of this precious moment, Caleb took one final step back. His form flickered gently, the light that surrounded him beginning to ebb.

"Goodbye, Riley," he whispered, his voice a soft breeze grazing her cheek.

In an instant, he began to dissolve into shimmering particles of light, cascading into the night like fireflies caught in the wind. She reached out, longing to hold onto him, but knew—deep within—the truth of their separation.

"Goodbye," she called, her voice breaking as she fought against the swell of emotion.

And as the final glimmers of light faded into the surrounding darkness, she clung to the strength of her memories and the indelible mark Caleb had left on her life. Here, at this lakeside, they would be forever entwined.

Tears streaking down her cheeks, Riley could already feel the heavy weight of sadness transforming into something lighter, something that echoed his final words. She would carry him in her heart as she returned to the realities that awaited her. A new journey lay ahead—not just for her but for the spirit of Caleb Whitaker.

15
picking up the pieces

Riley trudged through the front door of her suburban home, the familiar scent of cedar and lemon cleaner greeting her like a long-lost friend. Yet, the comforting smells carried no solace, only a reminder of the past. Camp Willowood felt like a distant dream, a fleeting moment now cast against the backdrop of her everyday life. The laughter and warmth of sun-drenched days were abruptly replaced by the stillness of her empty room.

She dropped her duffel bag on the floor and flopped onto her bed, staring at the ceiling. The memories flooded her mind like a torrent: the crackling campfires, the scent of pine mixed with laughter, the gazes exchanged under the stars—especially those shared with Ethan and Caleb. That last night, though bittersweet, felt sacred, filled with warmth that lingered even now. But as she lay there, a cold weight of loss settled in her stomach.

Riley rolled over and opened her closet to put away her camp clothes. As she rifled through the hangers, a flicker of something caught her eye. The wilted flower, the one she had carefully preserved, peeked out from a crumpled piece of paper in her travel laundry bag. It had been beautiful once—a white petal with hints of lavender grace, perfect against the backdrop of the night sky during the ritual.

Holding it delicately in her fingers, she felt the smoothness of the stem against her skin. The beauty had faded, just as the moments she cherished from camp seemed to slip away like sand through her grasp. Sighing, she tossed it onto her desk, a poor placeholder for the vibrant memories she carried. How was she supposed to resume the normalcy of school, of homework and clubs, when part of her was forever tethered to Camp Willowood?

She stood up and moved to her window, looking out at the fluttering trees just beginning to change with the coming autumn. The neighborhood buzzed with normalcy— children played in yards, dogs barked, and the scent of freshly cut grass wafted through the air. All Riley could focus on were the things she yearned for: the camaraderie with her cabinmates, the thrill of mysterious stories at twilight, and the connection with Ethan that had ignited but felt so abruptly put on pause.

Riley plopped back onto her bed, settling into her thoughts. The weight of her emotions pressed down on her chest like a brick. She missed camp and the feeling of being alive, of exploring the edges of life and the supernatural beyond. Most of all, she missed Ethan's easy laughter, the way his warmth enveloped her like a hug, and the connection that blossomed between them in that enchanted world.

The boredom of her room threatened to swallow her whole when the sharp chime of her phone broke the stillness. She gasped, feeling her heart leap at the sight of Ethan's name flashing across the screen. Riley snatched it up eagerly, her fingers trembling as she opened the message.

> Hey, Riley! Just wanted to say I've been thinking about you. I miss our talks and everything we experienced together this summer. Want to meet up soon? I'd love to discuss it all.

A flutter of excitement ran through her, invading her heavy heart with light. A part of her wanted to respond with equal enthusiasm, but self-doubt seeped in. *What if he had moved on? What if all that had happened under the campfire's glow faded away like the glow of the embers? What if their bond was merely a summer fling?* But as the warmth of his words seeped into her heart, she felt the urge to grab onto something, anything—a chance to reclaim the connection they had forged.

Riley hurriedly typed back, trying to sound as casual as possible.

> I miss you too, Ethan! I'm down to meet whenever you want.

As she hit send, she couldn't help but feel a rush of anxiety lacing her excitement. *What would they talk about now? Would they explore the ghosts of their lives outside together, or would they dissect the moments from camp, reliving memories that still felt raw?*

She glanced at the wilted flower again, a reminder of her unfulfilled promise to Caleb and the way he seemed to linger like a whisper beneath the surface of her everyday life. But for now, Ethan felt like a lifeline, the possibility of something new and vibrant amidst the heaviness of her emotions.

The next buzz of her phone made her jump. Ethan had replied almost immediately.

> How about tomorrow evening? We could grab some coffee and walk by the lake. It's supposed to be a beautiful night.

Tomorrow. Just thinking about it sent waves of hope cascading through her veins. She felt butterflies flutter in her stomach, and she smiled uncontrollably at the thought of seeing him again, the way he laughed, and the way his blue eyes sparkled when he smiled.

> Tomorrow sounds perfect! Can't wait to see you!

Riley set her phone down and leaned back into her pillows, allowing her thoughts to drift to Ethan. She envisioned him leaning casually against the coffee shop counter, his smile lighting up the dimly lit room. It was the reminder she needed to lift her spirits. The buzz of everyday life was still there, but now it swirled around her like leaves caught in a gentle breeze.

* * *

RILEY PUSHED OPEN the café door, a soft chime sounding overhead. The aroma of freshly brewed coffee mingled with the sweet scent of pastries, wrapping her in warmth. Sunlight filtered through the large windows, sending beams dancing across the wooden floor. It felt homey, inviting, reminiscent of lazy afternoons spent at Camp Willowood.

Her heart raced slightly as she scanned the room, searching for Ethan. A flicker of nervous anticipation coursed through her. It had been a while since they'd been face to face, and this was their first meeting outside the campgrounds, where everything had stirred a whirlwind of emotions.

Spotting him in a corner booth, she breathed a sigh of relief. Ethan lounged back casually, a lopsided grin forming as he caught her eye. He had that same easy charm she remembered—the kind that made her feel inexplicably at ease and excited all at once.

"Hey, you made it!" he exclaimed, motioning for her to join him.

Riley slid into the booth across from him, the warmth of his welcome washing over her like familiar sunlight.

"I wouldn't miss it for the world. I've been looking forward to this all week," she admitted, her voice brightening as she mirrored his smile.

They began to chat about the summer, recounting funny moments that had snuck up amidst the chaos. The way Ethan had twisted the campfire stories into comedic reenactments made her laugh harder than she'd thought possible. Each shared memory sparked inside her a flicker of nostalgia, a reminder of an unforgettable time spent under the broad, starry Michigan sky.

"Remember that time you challenged me to a swimming race? You thought you were going to win," Riley teased, leaning forward slightly.

Ethan chuckled, ruffling his sandy hair as if to shake off the playfulness. "I stand by my belief that it was rigged. How can someone swim faster when they're practically a fish?" he replied, feigning indignation.

"Please! A fish who almost drowned," she joked, and they both erupted in laughter, easing the lingering heaviness that had settled in the pit of her stomach since camp ended.

As their laughter faded, Riley's expression grew more serious. The reality of the past few weeks caught up to her, swirling around her mind like maple leaves caught in the autumn wind.

"Ethan, can I talk to you about something?" she asked, her voice wavering slightly.

"Of course. What's up?" His gaze softened, concern etched into his features.

Riley took a breath, remembering the weight of her experiences—the ethereal encounters with Caleb, the bittersweet memories that followed. "I've been trying to adjust to normal life again, and it's been... harder than I anticipated."

Ethan leaned back, a thoughtful expression crossing his face. "I get it. It was a lot to process. After all the campers left, there was a police investigation at Willowood. The whole place was filled with cops."

"What happened?" Riley asked, intrigued.

Ethan shrugged his shoulders. "They removed his body from the tree. They gave his family closure. You did good Riley—real good."

Riley smiled internally. It was good to know his family found peace too. "I want to do something more."

"What about starting a blog?" His suggestion was casual but deliberate. "We could write about our experiences at camp —the ghost stories, the legends—all of it. It can be a way to document everything we loved about it, and give Caleb the tribute he deserves. Plus, it would keep us connected to that world."

Riley's heart raced, a spark igniting inside her. The idea of crafting something tangible out of their unique summer felt invigorating, like breathing life back into the memories that both haunted and healed her. "I love that idea! We could even collaborate on spooky stories from other camps and connect with new friends who share that interest."

"Exactly! We can dive back into the lore, collect stories, maybe even run some school events once the year starts back up." He chuckled, clearly warmed by the thought of future adventures. "Think of all the crazy stuff we could share. It'll be like we never left camp."

A bright smile broke across Riley's face, her worries momentarily set aside. "I can already picture it. Thank you, Ethan. This means a lot to me."

Ethan's features softened with genuine happiness, reinforcing that same warmth she experienced throughout the summer. Their connection solidified in that moment, bridging the gap between the ghosts of the past and the hopes for their future.

As they exited the café, laughter still bubbling between them, Riley's fingers brushed against Ethan's hand, sending a pulse of warmth through her. He intertwined his fingers with hers, grounding her in the present.

"I missed you, Riles," Ethan gushed, twirling her body around until it landed on his. He pulled her close.

"I missed you too," she replied, exhilarated, wrapping her arms around his neck. "I'm ready for everything that comes next."

THE END

you might also like

escape the ordinary. find your spark.

Get swept away with Journey to Crystal Lake, a thrilling YA romance in two parts!

Maddie's annual camping trip takes a dramatic turn when a blizzard tears through the mountains, separating her from her family. Lost and alone, she finds herself in a deserted cabin... with Dex, the infuriatingly handsome boy from school who secretly holds her heart.

**Will they find their way back together, or will the storm ignite
a bitterness even fiercer than the blizzard?**

Part One!

Young Adult Romance

by Lia Lucas

Ebook & Paperback

snowbound with the boy next door

PART TWO

adventure awaits...

Maddie's annual camping trip takes a dramatic turn when a blizzard tears through the mountains, separating her from her family. Seeking refuge in a deserted cabin, she encounters the last person she expects – Dex, the infuriatingly handsome boy from high school and the campsite next door.

Sparks fly in the face of danger...

Forced to rely on each other for survival, Maddie and Dex's

contrasting personalities clash at first. But as the storm rages on, shared stories and flickering candlelight ignite an unexpected warmth between them.

Will their love weather the storm?

With dwindling supplies and no way to contact help, their newfound connection faces its ultimate test. Can their bond survive the harsh reality of their situation, or will it melt away like the snow?

Discover a captivating story of resilience, adventure, and unexpected love.

Part Two!

Young Adult Romance

by Lia Lucas

Ebook & Paperback

star-crossed rivals

opposites attract. or repel.

Avery's the golden child.

Noah's the rebel with a cause. They hate each other. But when forced to partner for the school's Shakespeare competition, their world collides.

Will sparks fly, or will their rivalry consume them?

Dive into a captivating tale of love, hate, and everything in between.

Opposites attract...or do they? Find out in this sizzling YA romance.

Ebook & Paperback

about lia

Lia Lucas is an emerging author of Urban Fiction, Young Adult, and Contemporary Romance. She has a wide range of writing interests and is currently living an incognito digital lifestyle.

Ms. Lucas is part of the Ardent Artist Books family.

Lia has published several books.

youtube.com/theardentartist
amazon.com/stores/Ardent-Artist-
Books/author/B08BX8F1DZ

also by lia

Y O U N G ◆ A D U L T

Journey To Crystal Lake - Part One

Snowbound with the Boy Next Door - Part Two

Star-Crossed Rivals

* * *

S E R I E S

The Haunted Hearts Series

Haunted Hearts - Book 1

Ink and Ashes - Book 2

Ghosts in the Attic - Book 3

* * *

18+ ◆ Adult

Curves

She Was Going Home

www.ingramcontent.com/pod-product-compliance
Lightning Source LLC
Chambersburg PA
CBHW071931150726
47999CB00001B/173